This girl tried to stare me down. It was very ambitious, considering her lesser number of eyes. I practically laughed. I had met thousands of dreamers. Some of them had enough backbone to try to stand up to me. A few even tried to stare me down. None were successful, so I met this teenage girl's gaze, fully expecting her to turn away. She didn't. Not one flinch or even a blink.

I certainly wasn't going to be the one to turn away first, so I tried to focus somewhere other than her eyes. That was hard to do because they were particularly spooky, especially for a human. Her pupils held a darkness all their own. Her irises were gray bordering on black, which was also the color of her nightgown and short hair. At first, I thought she wore black makeup under her eyes but then realized she just had dark circles there. Then I made the mistake of suddenly looking back directly into her eyes. Their intensity jolted me and I triple blinked.

I lost the contest.

If pressed, I would say that this made her happy. Not that she smiled. In fact, her expression remained unchanged, except that she raised a single eyebrow.

"You work for me now, Nightmare."

EMOTIONAL SUPPORT NIGHTMARE

A NYX & SHIVERS BOOK

PATRICK T. FIBBS

TALEHAVEN BOOKS

TALEHAVEN BOOKS
an imprint of Padwolf Publishing Inc.

www.talehaven.com

www.PatrickTFibbs.com

10-digit ISBN 1-890096-97-0, 13 digit 978-1-890096-97-7
Printed in the USA - First Printing

For Erin & Colin

1

My name is Shivers and I'm your worst nightmare. That's not just tough talk. It's my job description. As a night terror from the dream realm, it's my job to give wakers nightmares.

Hope we never meet, because I'll bring fear into your life. I pity you wakers, sleeping in terror. Personally, I had never known fear.

Although, technically speaking, I guess I do know Fear. She's my second cousin, once removed. But she's a very lazy nightmare and hasn't lived up to her name. Perhaps you've experienced her work—incredibly shoddy, bordering on lame. Fear relies almost entirely on tropes, like giant snakes or falling out of airplanes.

Fear may be family, but that doesn't excuse the lack of pride in her work.

What I should have said was I had never been absolutely terrified, not even by the Nightmare King.

A fourteen-year-old girl named Nyx forever changed that.

2

Nightmares don't get a formal introduction to their dreamers. There are no secret files that list all you wakers' greatest fears or easy-to-find terrors. Night terrors are expected to enter into a sleeping mind with zero preparation and just turn on the scary.

Not that it's difficult to figure out a dreamer's fears. Lots of you are already stressing and obsessing over things. A good nightmare can run with that. Still, a night terror has to be careful. Not everything lurking around in the human subconscious is exactly what it seems.

One time, this kid on my to-terrify list had a vision of a tarantula creepily crawling through this mind. Without bothering to investigate any further, I sent a two-story-tall tarantula into the kid's dream where it ripped off the roof of his house, exposing his bedroom to the night sky.

It was beautiful, with a full moon and eerie leafless trees behind the spider. Bits of house floated down into the bedroom. Acidic drool even dripped from the arachnoid's mouth and ate away a dresser and part of the floor.

It should have ended in screams and shivers. It didn't.

The kid wasn't scared. He was deliriously happy. It turns out his beloved pet of five years, Fluffy, had recently died and the kid missed his tarantula terribly. Seeing Fluffy come back, even as a twenty-foot-tall monstrosity, made the kid so happy he leapt up and hugged Fluffy around the neck, then hopped on its back to ride it around the dream version of his town like it was a pony.

The kid woke with a smile on his face.

I caught some agony on that one. Trust me, you don't want to tick off the King of Nightmares by making a dreamer happy because he'll do the opposite to you.

On entering the teenage Nyx's dream, I went straight to the back of her subconscious. Humans hide all sorts of fear and shame there.

It took some searching, but I hit paydirt. Shoved into a hole behind a dream couch that was then covered in hundreds of gallons of cement, there was an image of Nyx lying on her back on a redwood picnic table. It was no lazy day in the sun. Chains bound her arms and legs down.

Having learned my lesson after the Fluffy incident, I investigated her mind further, but there was nothing else I could find to explain why this would scare her. I was pretty sure humans didn't keep tables as pets and judging by the effort her subconscious went to bury this, the table terrified her.

Maybe she didn't like picnics. Could be she fell asleep and her friends tied her up with jump ropes and she got stuck there. There was no way of knowing the details, but there wasn't much else to work with in her mind. I mean, besides the typical fear of not fitting in with your peers. Nyx had that one pretty bad, but it's a pretty standard night terror for teenagers, but—unless you're my lazy cousin Fear—there's only so many times you can do the *I lost my homework and am standing in my underwear in the middle of English class* nightmare trope before it gets too boring to deal with.

You wakers have books, TV, movies, and the Internet. All we nightmares have are *your* dreams, so avoiding boredom motivates us to cultivate your fear for its entertainment value.

Don't judge me. If you were raised as a night terror, you'd be the same way. Don't believe me? Get rid of your phone, TV, and books (not this one, obviously) and see how long you last.

I set the stage for the terror to come. The first step was conjuring the picnic table, although I made some artistic changes. Black iron with jagged edges and spikes replaced the wood, and the chains were twice as thick as Nyx's torso. Had they been real, they would be too heavy for a human to lift but it did not matter because most of you wakers accept weird things like that in your dreams without questioning it.

Next, my power drew Nyx onto my stage. Her dream self appeared and came to awareness tied to my table. I stepped back and let her subconscious take over.

That's the beauty of my job. I could control everything in a nightmare, but I don't have to. You wakers are kind enough to let your minds do the heavy lifting for me.

Suddenly my spiked-out picnic table was the least scary thing in the room. A herd of people in dark robes with hoods that draped their faces in shadow appeared in a circle standing around the girl. They were holding hands and making noises. Not happy sounds like a campfire sing-along. These folks in the robes were chanting–Latin if I didn't miss my guess. That's one of the gifts of being a nightmare–you understand all human languages plus the languages spoken in dreams which often bore no resemblance to each other.

A tiny portal opened above Nyx. What it led to scared even me–it was a place too dark for even nightmares to survive long.

I'd never seen any dreamer's subconscious kick in this intensely before.

Two of the robed herd stepped towards the table, one on either side. The one to Nyx's left was a woman and the one to her right a man. From out of her left sleeve, the woman pulled a knife that was so dark it sucked up all the light in the room as she lifted it above Nyx. The man on the other side reached out with both hands to grab the hilt. The pair held the knife above her chest and chanted.

Nyx screamed at the sight, which made the two figures chuckle.

By the immaculate terrors, they were going to use it on the girl!

If she didn't wake up before they killed her, she'd die in the waking world too.

Plenty of nightmares would be getting their jollies right now, happy to risk the dreamer's life for their own amusement, the Nightmare King chief among them.

I struggle not to judge other night terrors for their sadistic tendencies. They rarely return the favor. Even as I stretched my purple tentacles out to grab hold of the dark knife to prevent it from plunging into the girl, I knew the King of Nightmares would be disappointed in me. His Majesty was jealous of those in the waking world and dedicated his existence to causing them any harm he could. It was the only time he smiled.

Me? This is just a job. The only one I've ever had. The only one I could ever have. But I don't hate wakers and I wasn't going to stand by and let one die.

I whipped a tentacle out and the snapping sound ended the dream and sent Nyx back to the waking world. She'd be terrified, but alive.

Still, petrified by fear counts as a win in my job.

If a night terror is around when a dreamer wakes, we get a brief glimpse into the waking world. As dreamers awaken, night terrors fade back to the Dream Realm.

As Nyx's eyes opened, I looked around her bedroom. Nothing too special. Basic bed, dresser, mirror. One thing was different–a rope hung from the ceiling. Maybe some teenage trend? I kept looking around to check out as much as I could before I faded and had to slither off to the next dreamer on my route.

Weird, I wasn't fading. I tried to move, but my tentacles stuck to the headboard.

I was caught in a net within a circle, the bottom of which was decorated with beads and feathers

Cute. A chuckle-worthy attempt of a dreamcatcher had me stuck in place. Those things are supposed to catch bad dreams before we get to the dreamer.

I had to admit, this one was better made than most—I hadn't even sensed it when I entered Nyx's dream. Your average dreamcatcher was no big deal to get out of. The mystic principle was sound, but this was just an arts and crafts project. To really snare us, there needs to be magic involved in the making, and that rarely happens. This cute little mesh had no more chance of keeping me trapped than it would of netting a great white shark if it was dropped in the ocean. I stretched out to thin my body and slipped away easily toward the girl's bed.

The instant my tentacles were clear of the dreamcatcher, Nyx sprang out of bed and yanked on the rope that hung from her ceiling.

What the figment?! Her blanket flew up and attacked me. No, not a blanket. I was hanging, stuck in a net that had been laid over the sheets and pulled up like an animal trap.

No problem. She was awake, so I'd vanish from the waking world in 3… 2… 1…

Why was I still in the net? I slithered to push my way through the ropes and continue on my rounds, except I didn't so much slither as flail about in one place.

The net was nothing like the arts and crafts dreamcatcher on the bedpost. It looked a little like a dreamcatcher, but the design was different.

I couldn't get out.

What a revolting development. Me, Shivers the nightmare, trapped and dangling from the ceiling in a teenage girl's room.

2

I flailed, squirmed, and undulated my tentacles, thinning out my body to squeeze through the tiny gaps between the ropes that made up the net.

Every time I tried, the gaps magically tightened, stopping me from getting through. I kept this up for almost an hour before I stopped, exhausted. The snare had somehow made me solid and visible in the waking world.

In the dream realms, I never got tired–after all, where would a living dream go when they slept? Having a physical body was exhausting. I don't know how you wakers do it.

As I lay there panting, Nyx got up from the beanbag where she'd been sitting and watching my failed escape performance.

We were eye to eye to eye. I had three at the moment, although one was not in a normal place, and hard to see if I didn't open it wide. I could easily manifest one or a hundred, depending on how I wanted to look. Same with my tentacles, but my normal form has nine.

This girl tried to stare me down. It was very ambitious, considering her lesser number of eyes. I practically laughed. I had met thousands of dreamers. Some of them had enough backbone to try to stand up to me. A few even tried to stare me down. None were successful, so I met this teenage girl's gaze, fully expecting her to turn away. She didn't. Not one flinch or even a blink.

I certainly wasn't going to be the one to turn away first, so I tried to focus somewhere other than her eyes. That was hard to do because they were particularly spooky, especially for a human. Her pupils held a darkness all their own. Her irises were gray bordering on black, which was also the color of her nightgown and short hair. At first, I thought she wore black makeup under her eyes but then realized she just had dark circles there. Then I made the mistake of suddenly looking back directly into her eyes. Their intensity jolted me and I triple blinked.

I lost the contest.

If pressed, I would say that this made her happy. Not that she smiled. In fact, her expression remained unchanged, except that she raised a single eyebrow.

"You work for me now, Nightmare."

4

She spoke in English, so that's how I answered her.

"I'd tell you to dream on, but this is the waking world, so you'd hardly be able to try. Give up your delusions. Nightmares don't do the bidding of humans."

"*You* will."

"Why would *I* do that?"

"Because you're trapped. And you'll never get out of my dream snare unless I let you out."

I strained my tentacles against the sides of the net but only held it for a few seconds. If an hour of struggling didn't do anything, a few additional seconds of effort wouldn't help.

"That's okay. It's rather comfortable in here." That was a lie. Having a physical form meant I could feel physical pain. Each strand of the net that touched me was like a live wire pulsing with electricity. "I'd be happy to hang around here for a bit. I've never had a vacation before."

The King of Nightmares would never allow it. I was lucky to ever get a lunch break.

"I'm sure, but having you hanging in my room would be too creepy, like having some twisted octopus piñata staring at me all the time." Nyx spun the net so I could see out her window. The moon was full and I could see a hole in the backyard with a pile of dirt and a shovel next to it.

"I dug you a new home where I'll bury you to enjoy your vacation. Then every month or so, I'll dig you up again and see if you're willing to take the deal I'm offering. If you say no, I'll throw you back in the hole and rebury you. Although I suppose it is possible if you said no too many times, I might forget or give up asking and leave you down there. Being buried alive, spending every moment in crushing darkness would be no big deal for a nightmare, right? You dish out worse before breakfast."

"Since most people have breakfast after they wake up, that's true," I said. Still, there were plenty of people who were terrified of being buried alive and the prospect didn't thrill me. In the old days on Earth, some people paid to have a bell above ground with a string that went inside their coffin. That way in case they weren't actually dead, they could ring it like their life depended on it in hopes that somebody would dig them up. I didn't think Nyx was going to offer me that option.

"It sounds quite lovely." If I had the curse of Pinocchio, my tentacles would've grown to three times their current size based on that whopper. It sounded terrible and I have to admit, the thought of it made me… unsettled.

Nyx must've taken me at my word because she untied the rope that was tethered to her ceiling and the dream snare dropped. It didn't hurt as I landed on the bed.

Although it wasn't pleasant when she grabbed hold of the top of the dream snare and pulled so that I fell from the mattress to the floor. Her dragging me out of the room to a hallway wasn't so bad, but her yanking me down the stairs so that I bumped and hit each one was more annoying than painful. My physical body as a manifested nightmare was still far stronger than a human body. I wonder if Nyx realized this.

She dragged me through another hall into a kitchen, then out a door to bump down three cement steps. We crossed more cement and then grass until I came to a stop next to the hole. Nyx was bent over with her hands on her knees grimacing as if in pain, saw me notice, and straightened up.

It probably wasn't a huge as holes go, but it was several times deeper than I was tall.

"I'll repeat my offer–you work for me."

This wasn't going well. Maybe if I can keep her talking to figure a way out of this.

"I hate to be that guy, but technically you haven't made me any offer. An offer consists of one party doing something for the other party in exchange for something else. You've offered nothing, so I can hardly agree to an offer I haven't heard, now can I?

Nyx's eyes rolled up a little as if she was looking at the sky as she stroked her chin.

"Fair enough. I need a night terror to help me out with a few things, mainly giving some people of my choosing nightmares."

That didn't sound too awful. "And what are you offering me in exchange?

"I'll free you from my dream trap."

With one of my tentacles, I stroked the bottom of my head where a chin might be if I had one. "That's a good start. What else?"

The girl was obviously well-versed in magic to be able to trap me like this. And her power worked against dreams. It certainly wouldn't hurt to have a little bit of magical protection should the Nightmare King ever decide to do more than punish and hurt me. Well, hurt me more than he usually did.

Nyx shook her head. "Nothing else. That's it."

"That's hardly enticing now, is it? How about rig up one of these dream traps that I can bring with me back into the dream realms. You do that and I'll continue negotiations."

Nyx continued negotiations all right, but her idea of making a deal involved her kicking me into the hole, picking up the shovel, and raining dirt down on me.

"Hey! You attacked me. I'm entitled to some compensation!"

"Wrong. You attacked *me.*" Nyx spoke through gritted teeth and for the first time, the tone of her voice changed. She sounded ticked off. "You invaded my dream and gave me a *nightmare!*"

I shrugged all nine tentacles at once. "That's my job."

"You think I enjoyed going through that again? What gives you the right to mess around with someone else's mind?"

"I refer you back to my previous statement. It's in my job description."

Her brows narrowed and her nostrils flared. "That doesn't make it right."

"Don't blame me. I didn't set up the rules for how the universe works."

"Well, then don't blame me for defending myself. If I leave you in there, you can't give your night terrors to another person. I figure that'll alone will make the world a better place."

Nyx more shoveled dirt over me as if it was a race. I tried to tough it out. If she wasn't going to speak, then neither would I. I managed to do it too. For a bit. At least until the soil covered all of me up to my highest eye. I managed to lift one of my tentacles and the net up out of the dirt. "Wait! I agree. With some conditions."

Nyx looked down at me, towering like a giant. "No conditions."

"But–"

The shovel started dancing through the air again as a storm of dirt poured down until only the tip of one netted tentacle could rise above the soil.

I coughed. "Fine. I agree." I was glad none of the other nightmares could see my embarrassment—a night terror defeated by a teenage human.

5

"Just don't hit me with the shovel when you unbury me."

Instead of an answer, I heard the whirling of a gas-powered mower followed by gale force winds blowing the dirt off my head and tentacles. I wondered if I'd be able to jump Nyx and overpower her when she jumped into the hole to pull me out. It turns out I never had the chance.

Nyx pushed a hoe into the hole, hooked the dream snare, and yanked me out, then shook her hands like they were bothering her.

Laying me on the ground, she pushed what looked like a dog collar towards me.

"What do you think you're doing with that thing?" I demanded.

"This will make sure you keep your end of our bargain."

"Oh no. I'm not some pet."

"I said no conditions." Nyx kicked my side, intending to knock me back into the hole but I was able to wrap my net-encrusted tentacles around her ankle and stopped myself from falling all the way in. "Fine. Put it on."

With a jerk of her leg, I shot back up to the grass and stayed still as she reached towards the bottom of my head, where a neck would be if I had one. The dream snare parted for her hands as if it wasn't there. A leather collar with metal studs around it wrapped around me. The girl in black put the strap through a metal buckle and tightened it. I felt a jolt of magic as it bonded to my skin as if it was part of me.

"So, little nightmare, tell me your name?"

Doing that would break the first rule of the night terrors. A nightmare that tells someone their true name gives that person power over them. Shivers isn't my true name, just the one I use.

I wasn't going to even give her that much.

"Myrtle."

I felt a mild tingle from the collar.

"That's not it. Try again."

"Shivers."

Nyx said "*Shivers.*" I felt a larger tingle from the collar. She shook her head. "That may be one of your names, but it is not your true name. Tell me your true name now or our deal is off."

I crossed two of my tentacles in front of my body, closed my eyes, and shook my head. When I opened my eyes, I was dangling over the hole again. Apparently, she needed my name to make the magic collar work even better at hurting me. Joy.

But all was not lost. Nightmare names are notoriously difficult to pronounce.

"You may have said no conditions, but I can only tell my true name to someone a single time. It would hardly be my fault if you can't remember it, but I still expect you to hold up your end of our bargain and not ask again. Deal?"

Nyx nodded. "Deal."

Despite every fiber of my now physical being screaming into my mind not to do it, I whispered my true name into the girl's ear.

I knew I'd be safe. The rule about only sharing my name once was real. My name had forty-seven syllables and only three vowels. It's not meant to be spoken aloud outside of the dream realms, especially through a human throat and mouth.

There was no way some goth teenager was going to hear it once and remember it, let alone repeat it.

Nyx must've known that. I realized too late she had black, wireless earbuds on, the type with a built-in microphone. She recorded my whisper on her phone. I watched as she opened up the file and played it back slowly. Her lips moved as she practiced the pronunciation slowly and silently for several minutes. She touched the collar again and correctly pronounced my name in its entirety. This time, the collar sent a jolt through me and constricted for a moment, choking me before relaxing to a comfortable position.

As she pulled the net open, she said, "So let's go over the ground rules."

I didn't wait around to hear them.

6

Except briefly when they wake, humans don't see nightmares in the waking world. The King of Nightmares is the only one I've even heard of that who can appear there whenever he wants.

The speed a cheetah or horse can achieve impresses humans. Now multiply that more than a few times and you'll have some idea of just how fast I can move. I figured any human watching me escape wouldn't have time to focus because I was moving so fast. In the space it would take one of you wakers to blink, I'd scurry out of your field of sight, never to be seen again.

I was so confident in my escape, that I dared to look back at Nyx. The human must already have come to terms with the fact that she was never going to catch me.

My tentacles have a rather elastic quality to them which allows me to stretch them out to great lengths. I reached out for a fence with a stretched tentacle, then leapt up and sprang toward the space above the tall pickets like I was a sling shot. Once gravity took over and pulled me down into the next yard, I'd be free. I celebrated by giving my former captor a salute with my middle tentacle.

She just rolled her eyes again.

7

Gravity didn't have time to kick in because something else smacked me down first. As I got near the backyard fence's airspace, it felt like I'd hit an invisible wall made of equal parts electricity and sledgehammers.

The shock threw me back to the spot I'd started from. The ends of my tentacles sizzled like calamari flambé.

Nyx came and stood over me. "If you'd bothered to wait until I told you the ground rules, it wouldn't have been so painful for you. At the moment, you can wander freely within the backyard and the house, but if you try to go any further than that, it's going to be quite unpleasant for you. Should we leave the premises, I can set the distance you can be away from me before the same thing happens."

If I couldn't get away, it left me with one other option. I rushed at the girl, leaping off the ground in a flurry of undulating tentacles of terror.

I smashed into another invisible wall, but this one was far worse. It felt like being struck by lightning while spun in a blender with blades made from piranha on radioactive expresso. My entire body sizzled and smoked.

It took several long and painful moments before I could move again.

"You didn't really think that I would design a control collar that would let you hurt me, did you?"

"I was kind of hoping," I managed to get out in a raspy whisper.

"I give you credit for trying. To be honest, I would've

been disappointed if you hadn't."

That revelation took me aback.

"So, in the interests of us having a good working relationship, I had the defense shield set on mild mode, so that if you tried it wouldn't hurt too bad."

Not hurt too bad? That was the third-worst pain I've ever felt.

Nyx pointed an index finger at the collar and twirled in a circle a few times. I felt a tingle where the leather touched my skin.

"I've now set the shields to maximum so I wouldn't advise trying that again. At least if you want to move around in the waking world under your own power. Now let's cause some nightmares, shall we?"

As Nyx spoke, the rosy foot of dawn tiptoed over the horizon, causing the girl in black to roll her eyes.

"Damn it. We won't have enough time before they wake up. We'll have to wait until tomorrow night."

Making nightmares was something I could deal with. I was good at it and–unlike having a physical body–it was familiar. The thought of the unknown that lay in front of me make my stomachs gurgle with anxiety.

"So what happens until then?" I asked.

Which is when I saw Nyx smile for the very first time. The sight sent chills crawling up and back along my tentacles.

8

Preparing for whatever new tortures my captor had in store, I followed her back inside a dark and empty kitchen.

My captor flipped a light switch to reveal a dinger bell of the sort humans once used at hotels to summon someone to a desk. Nyx smacked the top down three times, each hit followed by a crisp ding.

Down the hallway, two voices muttered curses and I heard people shuffling out of bed. One door now had a halo of light around its edges.

What some humans might consider an attractive older woman rushed out of the room, struggling to finger comb her blonde hair and tie her terrycloth robe at the same time. The robe was uneven and her hair remained a mess, although now at least most of the hair pointed in the same two directions

The woman stopped in front of my captor. She was all trembly and wringing her hands. I recognized the look of someone living a nightmare.

She smiled, but the fake grin couldn't even fool someone who wasn't human. It was too wide and didn't make her eyes crinkle. It looked as phony as one of Fear's attempts to make snakes in a dream. (My cousin's serpents look like cut up garden hoses with eyes and fangs. Barely startling from a distance, confusing up close.)

"So sorry, Nyx dear, for not being here when you woke. It is particularly early for a Sunday so I assumed you'd sleep in."

There was an odd sound and it took a moment to realize it was Nyx grinding her teeth. The woman bent forward with puckered lips aimed at my captor's cheek but then leapt back, her face contorted in pain and her skin smoking. It looked like Nyx also had shields in place to keep her mother at bay.

"Mother, you know touching me is against the rules. Why will you stop testing to see if my wards have stopped working. It will never happen. I'll excuse your tardiness this time."

Bowing, the mother scrambled backward trying to get away from her own daughter. "Yes, of course, dear. My deepest apologies. It must be the early hour and all the love I have for you in my heart that made me forget."

Nyx scowled at the woman who gave her birth and her mother withered under the girl in black's dark gaze. Nyx sat at the table. "Nice try. How about some breakfast?"

"Whatever your precious heart desires, my darling daughter."

Quietly from the floor, I observed the mother-daughter interaction. Although in dreams I could be as big as a house, my body in the waking world was about the size of a bulldog, but with all the tentacles, obviously far more handsome.

Nyx motioned me into a wooden chair at the table next to her. I slithered up and into the seat, laying two tentacles on the table's surface. The mother's pupils become quite large. She hid her fear quite nicely. Other than a few tremors in her fingers, it was barely noticeable.

"I see you've brought a friend with you. How lovely. A girl your age should have friends."

"I wonder why I don't have any," Nyx said with what I recognized as typical teenage sarcasm.

Joining in the conversation, I matched her tone. "*I certainly have no idea.*"

I expected a scolding or a jolt to my collar. Instead, the

girl with the black hair raised a dark eyebrow and smirked.

"So your parents are your servants?" I asked.

"My mother is a lawyer and my father a doctor when they aren't doing my bidding," Nyx said. "Shivers, since you're new to the waking world, what real food would you like to have for breakfast?"

I resented the implication that things in the dream realms were any less real than they were in the waking one because when wakers visit, everything they encounter is the realest thing they've ever seen. Even if they happen to be using a turtle as a combination remote control and toothbrush while it talks with the voice of their kindergarten teacher about the best recipe for a raspberry rainstorm. It doesn't matter that it wouldn't make any sense if they were awake. For that moment, that encounter has the highest percentage of reality they have ever experienced.

Still, the offer surprised and intrigued me. I've never gotten a chance to enjoy anything in the waking world. What nightmare had?

I thought about the foods I've seen people enjoy most often in their dreams before the screaming and tears begin. "I would like pizza and an ice cream sundae."

The mother glared at me as if she wished me dead. Perhaps she did. "Those are hardly breakfast foods."

"Anything you eat first thing in the morning is technically breakfast food," Nyx said.

The mother's smile enlarged but the fire in her eyes flared. "But daughter dear, we don't have either of those things in the house."

The mother's tone tried to pretend like it was being pleasant but as she spoke through gritted teeth it ruined the effect.

"Father, you've spent enough time hiding in your room.

Come out now," Nyx demanded.

There was some grumbling before a man came out in a fancy silk robe. His head was shaved bald and he had a pencil-thin goatee around his chin. By the time he reached the kitchen, the man had plastered on an even bigger smile than the one his wife had on her face.

"Good morning, daughter. I trust you slept well. I can't tell you how wonderful it is to wake and have your beautiful face be my first sight."

"It's getting deep in here. You keep talking and I have to put boots on so I don't get anything brown and stinky on my feet."

Like the mother, the father's smile didn't waiver, but his eyes squinted as he glared at his daughter. "Just calling them as I see them, you wonderful child you."

"Get dressed and go to the supermarket. We're going to have pizza and ice cream sundaes for breakfast."

The bald man's eyebrows shot up his forehead. The tiny hairs looked lonely on his bare scalp. "We? Are you letting your mother and I eat with you?"

The mother shook her head and pointed at me. Some humans consider that action rude. I didn't think it was so bad. Usually, when people pointed at me in their nightmares they were also screaming.

"The food isn't for us, dear. It's for Nyx and her new friend."

The father turned to look at me and his eyebrows tried to rise even further, perhaps hoping to land on the back of his head and escape. They weren't up to the task.

"What do we have here?" I remained silent and the father took this as an invitation to keep yapping. "I assume you don't go to my daughter's school, so where did you come from?"

"From a place where the merest shadow is darker than

your blackest night, where terror and fear rejoice, that is where I make my home."

"So you're from New Jersey then?" The man was making what I assumed to be a dad joke. I didn't find it amusing and it appeared no one else did either but the man still laughed at the attempt at humor.

I stretched four tentacles and rose to stare the bald human in his freakish two eyes. He simply looked me over from suckers to head.

"You have tentacles but you're dark purple which means you aren't from the shadow realm, so I'm going to guess you're a nightmare."

Impressive. Most humans had no idea that either nightmares or the shadow realm existed. Many of those who have information on the shadow realm either live in terror from the knowledge of the horrors that lurk just in a dimension just beyond their little world or they simply go mad from having gotten too close to dark things that only desire to torture and devour them.

Nyx's father wasn't even nervous, let alone scared. Interesting.

"It doesn't matter where my friend is from. What's important is that you're going to go out and get all the ingredients we need to make ice cream sundaes. Don't get all cute and bring back crappy ice cream flavors like coffee or you'll just have to go back to the store again."

"I would never be passive-aggressive like that." Nyx turned her stare on her father. He tried to match it but eventually crumbled, broke eye contact to look down at the floor. "At least not after what happened last time."

"It's good that you're learning. And don't bother getting frozen pizza. Get the stuff so mom can make the dough fresh."

"But daughter, that'll take a long time and be a lot of

work."

"It's Sunday, Mother. What else do you have to do?"

The mother opened her mouth as if to shout, but the father put his hand over her lips.

"Hush, dear, or your daughter might not think that she is the most important thing in your life."

That made Nyx snicker.

"I expect breakfast to be ready in ninety minutes so both of you better get busy."

Both parents bowed at the waist and said in unison, "Yes, daughter."

Nyx ignored them and turned to me. "Since we have a little time, you want to see my room?"

I tilted my head to the side. "Haven't I already seen it?"

Nyx got up and went to the refrigerator. She came out holding a cupcake in each hand.

"Nope. That was only my bedroom."

9

As I mentioned previously, we nightmares don't get scared. At least that's my story and I'm sticking to it.

I will however admit that I was a tad... apprehensive about exactly what was waiting for me in Nyx's room. After all, I was dealing with a fourteen-year-old girl whose favorite color appeared to be black and could not only trap a nightmare but give it physical form in the waking world.

That took power. The type of power humans rarely have. I was expecting all the room's surfaces to be as dark as night with maybe a pentacle painted on the floor. Perhaps even an altar set up for human sacrifice.

Her room was nothing like that. For starters, it was cotton candy pink and the only thing mildly resembling magic were a pair of black candles burning on a shelf in the corner next to the pinball machine.

Nyx spun around in a circle with her arms flung out to her sides to point at everything. Then I saw something that scared me–she was smiling again.

"What do you think?"

My head swiveled in two full circles to take it all in from the TV screen that took up an entire wall to a slushie machine with three favors. "It's not at all what I expected."

Nyx bounced up and down on her feet and hugged herself. "I know, it's great isn't it?"

I had to admit it was the perfect playroom for a lot of kids. More than a few adults too.

I nodded. "Your parents must give you a huge allowance

to be able to afford all this."

Nyx flipped the switch from what looked like a metal kettle and something started spinning inside of it. She picked up a pair of bare cardboard cones and one at a time put them in the kettle and moved them in circles. When she pulled them out, they were dressed in cotton candy. Although it didn't match the walls. It was blue.

"My parents don't believe in allowances or quite frankly, giving me anything." She held out one of the sugary clouds on a stick. "Want some cotton candy?"

I'd enjoyed the cupcake she gave me on the way in. "Sure."

I've seen cotton candy before. The number of people with nightmares about clowns might surprise most people. Things from the circus pop up a lot. It's rare that someone enjoys food in a nightmare. As a night terror, I experience things like taste and smell vicariously from the dream. It's been my experience that cotton candy tastes like pink house insulation, so I never understood why wakers willingly ate it. I nibbled a tiny bit into my mouth, expecting to be disgusted. Instead, the fluffiness melted on my tongues and an explosion of sweetness splattered my taste buds.

Cotton candy was fantastic!

I opened my mouth until it was wide enough to fit a human head inside and stuck the entire ball of fluff in my mouth and pulled it off the cardboard stick. I enjoyed another blast of sweetness like the last only this one was a hundred times bigger. Next, I ate the cone.

Nyx giggled. "You're not supposed to eat the cardboard."

"I see why. It wasn't very good. But the cotton candy was amazing."

Nyx plucked some cotton candy off her cone, squished it into a ball, then popped it in her mouth. "Want to play some foosball?"

"Are you going to punish me if I beat you?"

"Why would I do that? It wouldn't be very nice."

"But kidnapping someone from his plane of existence to do your bidding is?"

"You think I kidnapped you?" Nyx seemed genuinely surprised.

"What would you call it?"

"A rescue."

If I had a jaw, it would've dropped. "Why would you rescue someone who didn't want to leave where they were?"

"You literally live in a realm of nightmares, tortured constantly by the King of Nightmares."

"I wouldn't say tortured." Mainly because the King doesn't like what he does described that way and punishes anyone who uses the word.

"Would you be more comfortable with painfully punished?"

I shrugged my tentacles.

"Are you allowed to do anything you want? By that, I mean one single thing."

"Sure." Although I added in a whisper, "As long as I don't get caught."

"So, would you call it taking someone out of a situation where they're tortured and have no freedom a kidnapping or a rescue?"

When she put it like that, it was hard to argue the point. So I didn't. "So, no punishment or penalty if I trounce you?"

"Nope, but what makes you think you're going to win? You've probably never played foosball before."

"Maybe but there are 4 rods for each player to spin. You only have two arms. I can play all four rods at once not even using half of my tentacles."

"Bring it."

Before we started, we had to remove plastic coverings from the handles. "Is this new?"

"No. I've had it a couple of months."

"But you've never played it before?"

"I've never had anyone to play it with."

"None of your friends wanted to try it?"

Nyx's smile vanished, replaced with the scary expression she had when she first captured me.

"I don't have a lot of friends. Most kids think I'm weird. Or scary," she said, her voice barely a whisper.

"What about your parents?"

"I forbid them from coming in here."

"But didn't they buy you all this stuff?"

"Only because I made them. Besides, they've never wanted to play with me. After what they did, they're lucky I even let them live in this house. Or at all."

"Aren't parents the ones who are in charge of the children in the waking world?"

"Typically. But most parents, at least the good ones, also take care of their children. My parents did the opposite." Nyx took a deep breath and seemed to force her face back into a smile. "But enough about them. It's time for you to lose at foosball."

10

Nyx shocked me by somehow managing to beat me at foosball despite her puny number of appendages, although her hands became more clunky and slower the more she played. We stopped to have slushies. Mine was cherry, hers was grape. The sugary cold drink was even more delicious than the cotton candy.

We followed that up with a game of ping pong.

"How about we make things interesting and use more than one paddle?" I asked.

"It seems like that would give you a ridiculous advantage," Nyx said.

I swung my tentacle behind my back and tossed my paddle over my head where I plucked it out of the air with another tentacle. "I understand. It's only natural that you'd be scared to try."

Instead of getting indignant, Nyx chuckled. "That doesn't scare me. I'm a realist. You have more limbs so I'd have a very hard time competing."

"True, although you could just use magic to beat me."

Nyx shook her head. "Magic is dangerous. Especially mine. Using it to win a game of ping pong would be like using a missile to swat a fly. Sure, it'll get the job done but there's going to be a lot of collateral damage."

"You didn't have a problem using magic to capture me. Or make this lovely collar." I completely failed to hide the sarcasm in my voice.

"I hate to disappoint you, but it didn't take a lot of magic to make that snare. I started with what makes a dreamcatcher work and just improved the basic design. It was easy. And your collar didn't take all that much power to make either. I started with a basic dog shock collar and just magicafied the parts.

"Magicafied?" I said. "I've never heard that before."

Nyx shrugged and started tossing me ping pong paddles which I plucked out of the air. She again shook her hands as if the motion had caused her discomfort. "I guess I might've made the word up, but it describes exactly what I did."

"Where's the rest of my paddles?" I held six which means I still had three free tentacles.

"You'll have to make do with those. I only have eight and I'm keeping these two. Why don't you serve?"

Nyx tossed me a little white ball and I started the game.

It was no contest. While she beat me two out of three games in foosball, I had a clean sweep in ping pong, winning five games in a row.

Nyx was as good as her word and wasn't the slightest bit angry about losing. In fact, she was enjoying the game so much, she didn't seem to care.

11

"Breakfast!" yelled a voice struggling to be cheerful but sounding anything but. Nyx paused the video game we've been playing—*Joy Reaper: The Point of No Return*. "Let's go see how the meal prep went."

Even before we entered the kitchen, the aroma of tomatoes, garlic, and cheese that filled the air was overwhelming. It made my mouth moisten in anticipation of eating, which was a new experience. I'd eaten in the dream realms, but as I mentioned it was rarely an enjoyable experience.

Nyx's parents had slunk away to separate corners of the room and stood at attention with their backs along a counter. The father smiled, but the mother's lips trembled ever so slightly as Nyx sat at the table and inspected her culinary work. I took my place in the chair next to her. The pizza must've passed inspection as Nyx rolled the metal wheel of a pizza cutter across the melted cheese, but I noticed she had to use both hands and several tries to cut through.

Using a spatula, she put a piece on my plate first then a second on hers, but now her hands were trembling.

I lifted the slice, still hot enough to warm my tentacle pleasantly. I took a larger bite than I had when I first tried the cotton candy. The flavor washed over me. It wasn't sweet like the cotton candy or slushy, more of a tangy smooth mix.

Nyx smiled. "I guess you like it."

Not want to waste eating time by talking, I simply nodded as I took another bite. I've learned my lesson with the cotton candy which I'd devoured far too fast and savored each nibble.

Nyx folded her slice in half before biting into it.

Far too soon, my piece was gone, devoured deliciously.

"Shivers, would you like some more?" Nyx asked.

Without hesitation, I lifted my plate in front of me. "Yes, please."

Nyx put another slice on my plate, then on hers.

The mother cleared her throat. "Daughter, don't you think you've had enough? Do you really need to eat half a pizza by yourself?"

Nyx had cut the circular pie into four slices.

Nyx rolled her eyes and shook her head. "And why, pray tell, mother dear, shouldn't I have another slice of pizza."

The mother no longer seemed nervous but had a grin that some might describe as sadistic. "I'm only thinking of you, dear. You could stand to lose some weight, you know."

"I've lost quite a bit, not that you noticed. I seem to distinctly remember you and father feeding me high-calorie, unhealthy food for a long time. But I guess that was different since you were trying to fatten me up back then, weren't you?"

"I have no idea what you're talking about, dear."

"We both know that you're lying, mother. Now that the need for me to be a morsel for the Void has passed, you are happy to fat-shame me in order to undermine my confidence and self-esteem. A pity your opinion no longer means anything, isn't it?"

Nyx folded her slice and took a huge bite out of it, making a show of chewing and enjoying it while staring at her mother.

I may not be an expert on the subject being from the realm of nightmares, but something seemed very off about this family dynamic.

We finished off the pizza and Nyx turned to her parents. "Let's get this cleaned up and get the ice cream sundae toppings set up."

The parents leapt forward to follow her commands. The pizza plates were taken away and replaced with bowls, five tubs of ice cream, jars of butterscotch, hot fudge, marshmallows, strawberry syrup, cherries in a jar, and two cans of spray whipped cream.

"Help yourself," Nyx said.

I paused. "I've never done this before. How do I start?"

Nyx tossed the metal scooper with the bowl on the end towards me and I caught it. "First, scoop out whatever flavors of ice cream you want and put them in your bowl."

I took one scoop of each—vanilla, chocolate, birthday cake, cookie dough, and pistachio. Nyx did the same. Nyx held her bowl up and I scooped one of each for her.

"Next, add as much in as many toppings as you like." She demonstrated by putting hot fudge and some marshmallows over the top of hers. I tried each one.

She tossed me one of the whipped cream cans and kept the other for herself. She shook hers up, so I did likewise. Then she turned it upside down so the plastic tube part was above her sundae and she pushed the tube to the side using both her thumbs. Whipped cream poured out. And kept pouring out. She put so much on but it must've been five inches high. Finally, she put a cherry on top and handed me the jar. I poured the rest of the red fruit on top of mine.

There were two spoons on the table. Nyx kept one and push the other one towards me.

"Father, give Shivers eight more spoons."

Her father opened up the silverware drawer and did as instructed. I picked up one with each tentacle.

"And now we eat."

I watched her parents' faces grow pale as I opened up my mouth and rapidly shoveled spoonful after spoonful of deliciousness in. This was far better than the sweet snacks I'd had earlier. I ate so fast that the sundae was gone in moments.

An instant later, the cold caused my head to explode in pain.

Was Nyx trying to kill me?

The girl in black chuckled at my agony. "Relax, it's just an ice cream headache. They go away in a few seconds."

Nyx was right. Before I knew it, the pain vanished. Somehow, the hurt didn't take away from any of the deliciousness. I looked over to see that Nyx had only tried a few spoonfuls of her own sundae.

"Still hungry?" I nodded. She pushed the bowl across the table towards me. "You can finish mine if you want. If you eat slower, you shouldn't get the ice cream headache.

Following her advice, I used only two spoons which had the advantage of not only making this one headache-free but making it last longer.

12

"What did you think of your first full meal in the waking world?"

"I enjoyed it. Food in the waking world is much more flavorful," I begrudgingly admitted.

"I'm going to go take a shower and get changed. You relax. My parents will clean up and do the dishes. Don't you dare let them talk you into helping."

"Okay."

Nyx left me alone with her parents and what quickly became an awkward silence. The father kept staring at me and grinning while the mother looked as if she was afraid I was going to do something unpleasant like eat her.

It quickly became annoying, so I remained perfectly still for several moments, then sprang up onto two tentacles so my body reached the ceiling as my other seven tentacles shot forward wiggling like hyperactive snakes. Just for good measure, I yelled, "Boo!"

It felt good to be doing something normal like scaring wakers, even if they didn't seem to agree. The father spun and tried to run away, but instead smashed into the refrigerator. The mother screeched, fell to the floor, and crawled up into a ball, whimpering softly.

"Please don't kill us," begs the mother. I would've thought that adult wakers that had to live with Nyx would be made of sterner stuff than this. I'd seen five-year-old children act tougher during far more terrifying nightmares.

"I'm not going to kill you." I thought about adding "yet,"

but these two didn't seem to have a sense of humor and probably wouldn't understand that I was joking.

"Did our daughter tell you to murder us?" the father asked.

"Nope. Just not to help you with the dishes." They had heard that. "There seems to be a huge difference between letting you do chores and killing you. Why would you make that assumption?"

"Our daughter used her dark powers to enslave us. It's only a matter of time before she gets bored and ends our lives," the mother said.

"Heaven knows she's threatened to do it often enough," the father said. "Obviously, you can understand our predicament as it's one we share with you."

"How do you mean?" Sure, there was some debate as to whether I was kidnapped or rescued, but as long as I didn't try to go anywhere, I was fine. Nyx had been treating me nicer than anyone else had ever done in all of my existence.

"Isn't it obvious?" the mother said. "She's controlling you with a collar and if you step out of line, she'll use it to kill you."

"You're mistaken. The collar is not designed to kill."

The father laughed. "And how do you know that? Because she told you? Listen, Shivers, if you want to survive long around here, nightmare or not, you better wise up. Nyx is a master manipulator. She'll tell you what you want to hear, but the moment you step out of line–" The father smashed the palms of his hands together. "–she lowers the boom. At first, it's a punishment, but do it too often and you won't be around anymore. There are two dogs, three cats, a hamster, a hobo, and her own grandmother that are buried in the backyard that can attest to our daughter's homicidal nature."

She did try to bury me in the backyard but Nyx didn't seem the murderous type. Sure, she was scarier than I was, but she didn't come across as a killer. Her parents didn't come across as nice people, but I was hardly an expert on humans. How was I to know if they were telling the truth and not?

"If she's that bad, it seems to me that you two must be awful parents."

"How dare you try to blame us for our daughter being psychotic!" the mother shouted, only to have the father rush over and put his hand over her mouth.

"Hush, dear, she might hear you," the father said.

The mother's whole body started trembling. She nodded and the father removed his hand from her face. "Don't you think we tried to help her? To stop her sadistic streak before she could hurt anyone? We took her for counseling." She opened up a kitchen cabinet and pulled out a brown see-through plastic bottle with a white top and shook it in my direction. A bunch of pills rattled. "We even put her on medication to try to change her evil ways. What did we get for all our tender loving care? Magically enslaved, that's what."

"If that's the case, then where are your collars?"

"Our daughter may be murderous and evil, but she's very smart. Two adults walking around wearing collars would attract attention. What she did was much more insidious," the father said. "She mixed our blood into some wax to cast the spell that took away our free will."

The black candles in Nyx's room.

"You've seen them I assume?"

I nodded. "If she's as murderous as you say, why would she let you live?"

"As my husband said, she's far from stupid. She's a fourteen-year-old girl. Teenage girls don't get to live on their own. If something happened to us, who would put a roof over her head, food on her table, clothes on her back, and pay for her little playroom?" the mother said. "If we were to suddenly disappear, she'd get put in the foster care system and she doesn't want that. Instead, she enslaved us to go out and work for her during the day then wait on her hand and foot when we get home. You may think where you come from is filled with nightmares, but at least those only last until people wake up and then go away. Our nightmare is never-ending."

"So you're one of us now, one of Nyx's slaves. Welcome to our nightmare," the father said.

"If things are as bad as you say, surely there must be something you can do to get yourselves free."

"There isn't. The spell she cast forbids us from talking about it with any other people," the mother said. "You're not human which I suppose is the reason we can talk about it with you without the spell racking our bodies with pain."

That made sense.

"But maybe this time our daughter is not as smart as she thinks she is. Maybe we can work together to help free each other," the father said.

"What are you proposing?"

The father smiled. The sight made me feel queasy, like he was trying to sell me something. "A simple exchange. The spell prevents us from going into her bedroom or 'her room' as she calls it, but you're not under the same restrictions. If you can find and extinguish those black candles, we'll remove your collar and all of us will be free of her evil control."

"Okay. Take my collar off and I'll go blow out the candles."

The mother shook her head. "That's not how this is going to work. After all, we have no reason to trust you. How do we know that you won't just return to the dream world if we take your collar off and leave us here? And we'd be worse off than before we started because, make no mistake, our daughter will punish us for helping you get away."

"That trust thing works both ways. How do I know that if

I extinguish those candles that your hold up your end of the bargain?"

The father shrugged. "You don't but neither of us is going to risk our daughter's wrath unless we know we can get away before she can hurt us. So, if you want to be freed from the collar, you're going to have to extinguish our enslavement candles first," the mother said. "If you hurry, you could probably do it before she gets out of the shower. Then we remove your collar and all of us are gone before she's even dressed."

"I'm going to have to think about this," I said.

"Don't waste too much time," the mother said. "There's not much of it left."

"There's not much of what left?" came a voice from the doorway. I swiveled my head to see Nyx dressed in black sweatpants and a T-shirt, a pink towel wrapped around her hair.

"Ice cream. Your friend seems to have eaten most of it," the mother said.

"If Shivers wants more, one of you can just go out and get it. Doesn't look like you made any attempt to clean up in here. Shivers and I are going to go watch a movie while you two take care of this mess."

I swiveled my head back to see the parents both nodding like they were trying to convince me to blow out their candles.

Oddly, when we got to her room, the towel on Nyx's head was black. I didn't even notice her switch out the pink one.

Nyx had her own popcorn machine as well as butter and a half dozen different shaker toppings to put on it. From the way she treated her parents, I was expecting something along the line of *Alabama Machete Disco Slaughter Part 13*. Instead, we watched *Mary Poppins*, *The Wizard of Oz*, and *The Princess Bride*.

Working as a nightmare, I've seen people put into parts of hundreds of movies. It was weird to watch them on a screen instead of all around me, not to mention from beginning to end.

A few times I looked over at the candles, but Nyx didn't notice. I didn't go near them.

Later that night, the mother knocked on the room door. Nyx ignored her. She waited a minute and did it again. This went on for quite some time until Nyx finally got up and opened the door.

The mother tried to step in but convulsed like she was zapped. Her toes were smoking not unlike my tentacles when I tried to leave. She didn't strike me as stupid, so I think the girl in black was right. Her mother was testing to see if Nyx had taken down or changed the spell when she let me in. The mother did not look happy with her test results.

"What?!"

The mother forced the grimace of pain off her face. "I just wanted to check on you. See if I could help you."

"The last time you said you were trying to help me, I

almost died, so don't bother."

The mother's face and shoulders slumped as if the words had hurt her. Then her mouth opened wide as she laid her hand on her chest. "How could you speak that way to your own mother?"

"It's easy to tell the truth. At least for people who aren't you. Did you and Father finish the paperwork I told you to do?"

"Of course, daughter. We would never let you down. We emailed it to your principal and left copies on the kitchen table." The mother stood in silence as if she was waiting for a tip. Finally, she said, "What, no thank you?"

"After what you and father tried to do to me, not a chance. Ever. You should be grateful I allow you to be here at all. The two of you go to your room and don't come out until it's time to get up in the morning."

"Yes, dear," the mother said. "Good night, daughter. Good night, Shivers."

Nyx watched her parents march into their bedroom and close the door behind them.

"That seemed a little harsh," I said.

"If anything, after what they did to me, I'm being far too kind."

"What did they do that was so terrible?"

"What do you think?" she said, plopping back down onto the couch.

I shrugged. "I have no idea."

Nyx looked at me with her eyes squinted, as if trying to figure out if I was being serious. When she realized I was, she shook her head. "I don't want to talk about it. Besides, we have to get ready for the reason you're here. It's almost time to make some nightmares."

14

I don't think the three dreamers could have screamed any louder, but that didn't stop Nyx from trying to make it happen.

The girl in black had talent. The King of Nightmares was lucky she was human. If she was a dream, she'd give him a serious run for his crown.

What had these three boys done to upset my captor? I had no idea, but it made me want to make sure I was never the object of her wrath.

The dream started out simply enough. Three teenaged boys beginning a normal school day. Some of the best nightmares start out as common activities. It lulls the dreamer in with a false sense of safety before dropping the terror into their laps.

What was much more unusual was Nyx insisting I link the three wakers, so they experienced the same dream. Not that it doesn't happen naturally on occasion. It's just rare, like finding a four-leaf clover or someone standing in front of a dream class wearing all their clothes.

The trio was walking down a hall, laughing, and telling jokes that would only be funny in a dream. This one was about the horse DJ in their math class and her problem with gumdrop moth soup leaking out of her ears onto the turntables when she played the Pythagorean Theorem dance remix. You had to be dreaming to get it.

They approached another kid, this one skinny and standing with a slouch. His arms were so thin in another dream someone might try to take them off and stick them in the side of a snowman instead of using branches.

The drama began when the trio approached the frail boy.

"Get over here, geek," ordered the largest of the trio. His letterman jacket had the name Steve stitched on it.

Realizing he'd attracted their attention, the frail boy turned and fled.

"Don't be like that, Irving," said a dark-haired boy whose letterman jacket stitching identified him as John. "We just want to talk to you."

Irving wasn't buying it and sprinted faster, which truthfully was at a rather pokey pace.

"It's only going to be worse for you if you run," said the third boy. He was the shortest of the three but that still put him a head and a half higher than Irving and probably three times as wide. If his stitching was to be believed, his name was Chuck. "It's only going to make it worse when we catch you." Instead of stopping, Irving rounded the corner. Chuck and Steve chased after him while John split off and ran a different way.

The frail boy's escape attempt was cut off by John, so he spun around only to see Steve and Chuck bearing down on him. Irving tried to duck into a classroom, but the doors were locked.

At this point, I should probably mention of the part of Irving was being played by quite possibly the handsomest of all nightmares—yours truly.

Was I bragging? Perhaps, but my acting skills are phenomenal. If I could compete, I'd win the Oscar, Tony, and Emmy every year for best actor. No human could compete.

With "my" back against the locked door, Irving me slid down to the floor, cradling books to my chest as I curled into a fetal position.

"Why don't you guys just leave me alone?" I whined in a

nasal voice.

"Because you're so much fun to hang out with," Steve said.

The frail boy I was pretending to be grinned maniacally yet appearing still very nerdy. A very hard combination to pull off believably. "You know something? You guys are right. I am fun."

I reached out with three—yes three—arms and grabbed hold of the bullies' ankles. Being a dream none of them questioned the extra limb as I lifted and flipped them over to dangle in front of me

My arms morphed into tentacles as my body grew until I was two feet taller than any of the bullies and I swayed their bodies side to side, narrowly missing smashing them into each other.

"You know what, Irving buddy? We may have misjudged you. How about you put us down?" asked John.

A fourth tentacle stroked my chin. "Nope. That doesn't really work for me."

Instead, I spun the three of them around like an amusement park ride and their screaming started. If they were in the waking world, vomit would be flying everywhere.

Then I grew, smashing through the ceiling of the school until I was fifty feet tall. I swung them above the ground when suddenly another giant appeared next to me—

Nyx.

But, at her suggestion, I had made some changes to her appearance besides being a fifty-foot-tall girl in black. Her hair moved like it was made of shadowy snakes, her mouth was full of giant shark teeth, and her black fingernails spun and groaned like chainsaws.

"You guys made a mistake picking on Irving," she bellowed, the scream making even my body tremble and vibrate.

Nyx took the three bullies from my tentacles and started

juggling them through rings of fire and blades that had sprung up in the dream sky.

I was impressed and a little jealous when Steve, John, and Chuck screamed far louder for Nyx than they had for me.

After a moment the flying fire was joined by floating water filled with ice and electrical mini-sharks. As she threw the bullies into the air, they passed through alternating fire and ice as the sparking sharks took tiny nibbles out of their hides.

"I want you to remember this the next time you even think about hurting my friend Irving," Nyx shouted, then tossed the bullies hundreds of feet in the air where they hung for a moment like cartoon characters. They reached out and clung to each other. They even stopped screaming, thinking their collective nightmare was over.

It wasn't.

Instead, they plummeted at speeds a jet would have a hard time matching and the screaming started anew. They looked down and saw my version of Irving's face looking up, which confused and maybe calmed them. They still had the idea that maybe Irving wasn't so scary but when I opened my maw, it revealed thousands of undulating teeth swimming in shadows. Each tooth had a mouth on it with another mouthful of teeth, each of which had another mouth and teeth, repeating the pattern as they headed down toward the depths of infinity. The sight made the terror return along with even louder shrieking.

And they kept screeching as they fell into my throat which had become a bottomless pit of endless despair and eternal darkness. The bully trio kept falling through the devouring darkness until mercy allowed them to wake up safe in their beds, sweating and screaming for their mommies.

15

"Great job, Shivers," Nyx said.

I didn't respond for a moment. I'd never gotten a compliment for my dreamcraft before. I wasn't sure of the protocol.

"Sure," I finally said.

"Time for me to get some Zs."

To me, it seemed unnatural watching Nyx prepare to sleep, although I'll admit to a personal bias here. Having spent my entire existence until yesterday in the Dreaming, I'd never had the need–or for that matter, the desire–to sleep. It seemed nine kinds of wrong.

Although it embarrasses me to admit, I found the entire process fascinating. I watched Nyx climb into her bed, fluff her pillows five times, lay down on her side, and pull the covers up to her chin.

"Good night, Shivers."

"I suppose it was," I admitted. I'd had fun.

Nyx gave a snort of air that seemed about halfway to a chuckle. "That's just something people say to each other before they go to sleep."

"So you'd say bad night if it wasn't good?"

Nyx pushed herself up onto her elbows and looked at me. "It's not so much a statement of how the night was up until that point. It's more of a wish on how the rest of the night should go."

"But the rest of the night isn't going to go anywhere. You're going to sleep."

"It's a phrase that has multiple meanings I suppose. You're wishing the person gets enough sleep so they don't wake up tired, that it's restful, and they don't have any bad dreams."

"Seems a rude thing to say to me. After all, I literally am a bad dream."

Nyx shook her head. "I don't think that you are. Sure, you're a nightmare, but it's what's inside that counts. I think inside, you're good."

"I've spent my entire existence giving nightmares and terrors to people. How could I be anything other than bad?"

"The entire nightmare thing is what you do, not who you are. I watched you give that trio of losers the dream I asked you for. You could've done a lot to make things worse for them, but you didn't. In fact. you almost looked like you felt guilty."

"No nightmare worth his weight in terror is going to feel guilty for scaring a waker."

"No reason why you should as you're actually helping some of the people you scare."

This girl may have been crazier than I first thought.

"How is scaring somebody going to help them?"

"I'm not saying you're helping everyone, especially if you're making someone relive one of their worst or most traumatic moments of their lives." She seemed to scowl at me but then stopped. "But an average, run-of-the-mill nightmare could help someone release stress or confront a problem they're afraid of or were ignoring. True, it could have the opposite effect. It's definitely situational. Deep down, I still think you're nice."

It was my turn to laugh. "You're way off there, missy."

"Am I? Did you spend the day trying to figure out how to scare and terrify people or did you just hang out and have fun?"

She was right. What was wrong with me?

"Well, we weren't in the realm of nightmares and I don't have anywhere near my full powers here in the waking world."

"True but you're a creature with tentacles that can contort and change his body shape. At the very least you could've scared my parents. Which mind you, I would've been okay with. Instead, you acted just like a regular person."

"That's the second time you described me as a person. I'm not." Terror knows the Nightmare King has told me that often enough. "I look a lot like one of your waking world's octopuses."

"You're not human but I don't think that's what defines a person. I think it's what is within their heart that does."

"The only thing in my heart is purple blood."

"Just because you tell yourself that doesn't mean it's true."

"Oh and I did scare your parents, but it was just a little one," I said. "See, I knew I liked you for a reason. I've really enjoyed spending the day with you, but I have to go to school in the morning so I need to be rested. Feel free to entertain yourself. And I hope you enjoyed our day too."

I started to make a snide remark about how awful it had been when I realized I actually did have fun. Fun outside of scaring isn't something I'd had a lot of experience with. I swallowed my words and nodded.

Nyx laid back down, returned her blankets to their original position, flipped her pillow so the cool side was up, and closed her eyes.

Her breathing slowed, her eyes did a rapid twitch, and at one point her body convulsed.

As I watched her, I realized I was feeling something new. I was lonely.

In a voice so soft it made a whisper seem like a shout, I said, "Good night, Nyx."

16

I've never really given much thought to how things were for wakers when they weren't asleep. There was no reason to.

But I did quickly figure out why sleep was so important to humans–boredom.

I could do was whatever I wanted and I had no idea what that was. I wandered around Nyx's room. I looked through some books, picked up a few stuffed animals which I expected to be creepy but were just stuffed bears and unicorns.

Maybe it would have been different if I wasn't magically fenced in one house where I was trying to be quiet so I didn't wake the humans up. I didn't know how to deal with so much free time. I'd never had any before. The Nightmare King doesn't exactly let you clock out for coffee breaks. His Majesty expects all his little terrors to constantly be frightening dreamers. And since there was always somebody sleeping somewhere in your world, this was theoretically possible.

There were plenty of nightmares that did just as they were ordered. The order followers soon became husks, devoid of any personalities of their own, existing only to follow the commands of the Nightmare King.

Me, not so much. I snuck off whenever possible. That's not free time, it's stolen time. Not the same at all. I always had to be alert for the Nightmare King or one of his spies. The trick was to hide in somebody's dream because then you could claim you were working.

Unless he was focused specifically on that particular dream, His Majesty had no way of knowing for sure. There are billions of you wakers, simply too many for the Nightmare King to keep perfect track of.

There are some lovely dreams out there, like riding on unicorns or hitting the winning home run in a baseball game. I like those. Usually, I sit in the stands and eat bland dream popcorn or hotdogs. Still better than working.

In Nyx's house, my activities were far more limited. I went to her room but didn't want to watch another movie or start a new video game. Playing a board game by myself seemed rather pointless. I could play ping pong by stretching myself so I had tentacles on each side or try pinball, but the noise might wake Nyx and her parents up.

I went back to watch her sleep. I tried to get into her sleeping mind but the collar stopped me. I didn't want to do it to frighten her, just to hang out. It had been the best day of my existence. Nightmares didn't have friends. Sure, I knew other nightmares who I occasionally spent time with, but even then we were supposed to be working.

There was no family either. At least not any that cared.

When I was two days old, my own mother gave me as a gift to His Majesty. Nightmares are born able to talk and get around, but I was still just a kid.

I still was. I probably was about the same age as Nyx. There are no child labor laws in the nightmare realm.

I returned to her playroom and sat in the darkness. Not on the floor or furniture, mind you, but on the ceiling. The suckers on my tentacles worked like tiny suction cups which let me walk on whatever surface I wanted. I can see perfectly well in the dark too, but the room was lit by those two black candles.

The twin flames were still burning, but neither hunk of wax looked any smaller than they had this morning.

I thought about what the mother and the father had asked. I'd be lying if I said I hadn't thought about blowing out the candles a dozen times. It would be nice to be free, but the more I thought about it, the more I realized my situation wasn't really that bad.

I had to create one nightmare, which was fun. I didn't have to hide or get punished by the Nightmare King. Plus, I got a chance to spend time with someone who was nice to me. That would never happen back home unless a dreamer confused me for someone they knew. And then, it wasn't really me they were being nice to, was it?

Just two little puffs of air and I'd be free. But free to do what? Go back to the nightmare realm? That option wasn't appealing. Unless the parents got my collar off, I might not even be able to go back.

I was able to go into those three bullies' minds and link their dreams without being in the dream realms, just on the border. That meant I might have other options available but shriek me if I knew what they were.

Maybe I should go into the mother and the father's dreams, just to watch and get a little insight into what the truth is. Although dreams don't necessarily show you what a person's character is. Good people can do bad things and bad people sometimes do nice deeds.

I couldn't quite figure out the relationship between Nyx and her parents, but considering my own mother gave me away as an infant, I don't have a lot of experience with the child-parent dynamic. I stared down at the twin flames and decided to let them keep burning. Not because I was afraid of the consequence of Nyx punishments. The real reason perturbed me.

I didn't break the spell on her parents because it would make Nyx sad. Why should a nightmare care about whether a waker girl was sad, happy, or singing in the shower? I didn't know.

But it was reason enough.

17

Morning took its time coming around which was very annoying. I was used to the Dream Realm where the time of day can change in an instant, then change back.

I'm not sure how all the waiting for things to happen in some stupid order doesn't drive humans mad.

Nyx's juggling of the bullies had looked rather cool, so I spent much of that time teaching myself the skill. After mastering juggling, I practiced maneuvering around with my tentacles. Yes, I've had tentacles my entire life, but in the dream realms, I can float or fly if I want to. Here in the waking world, not so much.

Physics sucked.

I stretched my tentacles then contracted them which pulled me from wall to wall. I even learned how to flop and flip myself up and down the wall, as well as go sideways around the room quite rapidly. I went outside, careful to stay in the backyard. If I stretched my tentacles that were on the ground and reached one up into the air, I could latch on to the house's chimney and fling myself over the building in a single bound, sort of reverse bungee cord jumping. It wasn't flying, but it beat walking or slithering.

The sun came up, but the humans kept sleeping. What was wrong with them?

After there had been daylight for more than half an hour when an alarm clock blared from the parents' room. It was followed by mumblings and grumbling that weren't quite as loud.

The mother and the father came tiptoeing out of the room. They stepped especially gingerly as they came to Nyx's door. The pair stopped with their hands raised as if they were going to touch the door. They stood frozen in place for an instant before scurrying into the kitchen, their eyes darting from the ceiling to the floor then to the walls.

It was obvious what they were scanning for.

"Looking for me?" I asked from my perch on the wall next to an old-fashioned landline phone.

The father spoke first. "You didn't do it. Why not?"

"How do you know?" I asked.

"It's easy to tell. Trust me," the mother growled.

They had tried to get into her room and couldn't.

"It was such a simple request. It would take you the briefest of moments to free us. What's the problem?"

I tilted my bulbous head and squinted two of my three eyes at the mother. "I don't owe either of you an explanation."

"So you're happy being a pet on Nyx's leash?" the father asked, pointing to my collar.

Before I could answer, the mother let out a shriek and collapsed on the wall, her head resting on my short body right below my head. Her shriek was followed by the leakage of salty tears from her eyes that dripped onto my skin. It was disgusting, but somehow my body seemed to like and absorb the moisture.

Her sobbing didn't stop, so I looked towards the father hoping he might drag his mate off of me. The bald man didn't. Instead, his lip trembled as a single tear drizzled. It was soon followed as others dribbled down his face. His face and body had stiffened as if he was fighting to hold something back. He wasn't very good because a moment later he to collapsed onto the wall next to his weeping wife, his head alongside the front of mine. His fight lost, he gave up any pretense of hiding or holding back his emotions and he too began weeping, adding his tears on my skin next to those of his wife.

That's when things got even more disgusting as snot leaked from his nose onto me.

I wanted to grab each of them with a tentacle then throw them across the room, but I didn't. I didn't know my own strength yet, but I was certain I was much stronger than a human being. I wasn't sure if Nyx would be mad at me if I broke her parents. In my experience, people crying in nightmares searched out a loved one, parent, significant other, or friend to comfort them while they cry. This often involved hugging and other physical interactions.

Why these people had chosen me was a mystery. Wanting to get this awkward dripping of fluids off my hide as quickly as possible, I lifted a tentacle for each of them and patted their heads, shoulders, and backs.

I must have been doing it wrong because it only slowed their crying and didn't get either off of me.

"What you're doing!?" screamed Nyx from the doorway of the kitchen.

18

That certainly made the parents get off me. In fact, they leapt backward as if Nyx's words struck them with a bolt of lightning.

"Those are the two most horrible and evil people in my life! How could you hug them? You never even hugged…" Nyx stopped short, her voice sounding like she couldn't decide if it should crack or cry.

"We were just telling Shivers about all the horrible things you do to us and he was kind enough to comfort us," the father said.

"And Shivers is such a good hugger. I feel so much better now," the mother said, not even trying to hide her smirk.

"I can't believe you would hug them."

"In all fairness to me, I've never hugged anyone in my life. The two of them were crying on me, getting tears on my skin, and both wouldn't get off of me, so I did what I'd seen dreamers do and tried to comfort them so they would stop crying and get away from me."

"It sure looked like hugging to me," Nyx said.

"Oh, it was," the mother said. "And with all those tentacles, Shivers is simply the most magnificent hugger ever. It certainly helped ease the pain of this life you've forced upon your father and me."

"I think you meant to say that I let you live. I didn't have to you know," Nyx said.

"We know all too well, daughter, that you could've killed us like you did our friends," the father said.

"I've never killed anybody and you know it."

"Do we?" the mother said. "Because you could have made sure our friends didn't die, but they're dead anyway."

"That sure sounds like killing to me," the father said. "Are you going to kill your little friend when you get everything you want from him?"

I didn't think a nightmare could die. But what do I know? Not much. At least that's what the Nightmare King has always told me.

"I. Am. Not. A. Killer!"

"So you say, dumpling, but all those corpses that happen to drop all around you might argue the point," the father said.

"If dead bodies could speak," added mother.

"True, they usually don't, but they could if our daughter here used her power to make them," the father said.

Nyx looked about ready to rip off somebody's head. "I can't bring someone back to life. It would just be a twisted puppetry of their bodies."

I thought that would make an awesome nightmare but kept that thought to myself.

Nyx turned to glare at me, her eyes bulging out in anger like at any moment they might pop out of her head. Where I was from that was not only possible but common. I still wasn't sure if it could actually happen in the waking world or not.

The room got darker as Nyx screamed at me. Something seemed to block the sunlight from the windows and the brightness from the lights. "How could you comfort and be nice to them after everything they've done to me?"

I held my tentacles up in a non-threatening gesture. "I was just trying to get them and their salty face juices off me. I didn't want to hurt them…"

The father cut me off. "Any more than we'd already been hurt by our own daughter."

The shadows in the room seemed to grow. Was that a thing in the waking world? "You're taking their side over mine?"

I shook my head. "I'm not taking any sides."

"Because he's too afraid of what you'll do to him. After all, you've already enslaved him," the mother said.

"You think Shivers is enslaved?"

The father nodded. "He's wearing a collar that punishes him and traps him on our property. If that's not enslavement, then what is?"

Nyx spun back towards me, the expression on her face angry enough that I crawled backward up the wall until my head was touching the ceiling.

"After what we talked about, after everything we've done together, do you think you're enslaved?"

Nyx was getting angrier each time her parents spoke. Anything I said would likely only make things worse. "Well…"

"You can't ask an enslaved person if they think they're enslaved. How are they going to answer you? Shivers is probably terrified that if he says the wrong thing, you'll use the collar to punish him. Daughter, you know the truth. Do you think because you gave him some junk food and played a few games with him that it excuses what you've done? Don't delude yourself. We taught you better than that."

"Sorry, Daughter, but using your power to control someone isn't going to turn them into your friend. It's obvious that like any decent, normal person, Shivers likes us more than you," the father said.

"And he would rather spend time with us than be miserable with you," the mother said.

That wasn't true! Before I could tell Nyx, her voice exploded in my direction.

"Is that so? Fine. You're a horrible, disgusting creature. I can't believe I actually liked you."

She liked me? No one's ever liked me before. I tried to tell her but she never even took a breath.

"I can't believe I thought we were friends."

"You did? I've never had a friend." Nightmares were lucky if we had acquaintances.

"Go ahead and laugh at how naïve I was."

"I don't want to laugh."

"Because I'm so pathetic? So stupid? So easy to fool? I'm nobody's fool. You think you're enslaved now? You have no idea. You cannot talk to or touch my parents. As soon as I'm done with my shower, we're leaving for school."

Nyx turned to her parents. "The two of you get on your knees, bow your heads, and freeze there until after we've been gone for fifteen minutes. And you can't speak to Shivers either."

Nyx stormed down the hall—actually she was moving slowly, practically limping—and into the bathroom then slammed the door behind her.

Light returned to the kitchen.

19

As I froze in the corner between the wall and the ceiling, I watched the parents get on their knees and stay there. However, I could still move, but I didn't want to. I was more miserable than I ever was before, including that time the Nightmare King locked me in a box with a pair of conjoined crocodiles, a hundred scorpions, and the Drooling Clown.

Only in the last day and a half had I ever been happy and had what I thought might turn out to be a friend. Both had been unthinkable in the nightmare realm.

My existence had been awful before, but I hadn't realized how horrible until I was presented with something better. Nyx dangled hope in front of me, let me touch and taste it, then yanked it away.

It made going back to being miserable a hundred times worse. This was worse than wretchedness. I'd never expected anything good from anyone so I could never be betrayed before.

Nothing mattered anymore. If I stayed with Nyx, I'd be ordered about, teased by the memories of something better. If she freed me, with nowhere else to go, I'd probably end up back in the realm of nightmares, tormented by His Majesty for the rest of eternity.

I can't believe a few hours ago I cared about not making Nyx sad. Now I wanted to make her hurt like she hurt me.

There was one surefire way of accomplishing that.

I slithered out of the kitchen into the hall. While

practicing getting around during the night, I learned that my tentacles had different sound modes.

The first let every sucker coming loose make a sound that was a cross between a drop of water plopping into a bucket and a wet slopping popping sound. Done slowly it was deliciously creepy. Coming from a nightmare, that means something because I know creepy.

The second mode was so quiet it would make the best dream ninja sound like an elephant stomping around in snowshoes by comparison.

It was child's play sneaking past the closed bathroom door and into Nyx's private room.

From the ceiling, I reached down and turned the doorknob, and rolled my body and tentacles right over the top doorjamb.

I reached one tentacle to the opposite ceiling and let it snap me across the room. Stretching a tentacle, I lowered myself upside down like a spy stealing a diamond until I dangled in front of the twin black candles.

I hesitated but only for a moment. I inhaled deeply and then let out two quick puffs of air. The flames died and the room went dark.

20

I returned to the kitchen even faster than I left by reaching a single tentacle down the hall to the ceiling inside the kitchen and snapped myself down the hall. I landed on the kitchen ceiling in time to see the mother and the father get up from kneeling to dance then hug each other.

They stopped long enough to look up and smile at me.

"Thank you for freeing us," the father said.

"You can thank me by getting this collar off."

The mother smiled and opened up a kitchen drawer and started rummaging through screwdrivers and spatulas. "Of course. And after we do that, perhaps we can interest you in a little evening up of the scales."

Before she could tell me what that meant, the bathroom door opened. The mother quietly shut the drawer and the parents dropped back to their knees with their heads bowed.

Without thinking I snapped a tentacle out and landed on the wall where I'd been when Nyx left.

Nyx sped into the room, dressed in pink tights and a pink long-sleeved dress covered in rainbows and unicorns, a sharp departure from her normally somber color scheme. She wore a black backpack, however.

Ignoring her parents, she walked by like it hurt her to move. When she reached the back door, she turned to glare at me.

"Let's go," she ordered. I slithered across the ceiling lowered myself down from the ceiling right side up so I could look her in the eyes. "I don't think I should go with you to school."

"Why not?" Nyx demanded.

"You mean besides the fact that a creature resembling—but not quite the same as—an octopus will stand out among you wakers?"

"I've already got that covered."

"Well, if dreams are to be believed, high school is one of the most terrifying places on Earth." People in their nineties still have nightmares about it.

"Yeah, high school is scary. So what? If I can deal with it, so can you. Got anything else?" Nyx said, putting her hands on her hips and bending forward at the waist so her stare was brought closer to my face.

"How about I just don't want to go? Does that count for anything?"

"Last night it would've but then I would've told you the two of us would've had fun together. Today, I don't care about your feelings. Why not try telling the truth. You want to stay here so you can spend more time with your two favorite people."

I blinked twice because it took me that long to realize she meant the parents. I still didn't like either of them, but if I stayed they could take my collar off and I could get on with the getting gone.

"You're going to school with me and that's final." I could see the mother—still kneeling on the floor—waving me away with her hands. I reached a tentacle over and opened the door, reached another one to a tree, and swung myself outside.

Nyx followed me, slamming the door behind her.

"That swinging is new."

I reached to the front corner of the house and snapped myself forward so I was on top of the drainpipe. "Everyone else was asleep. I needed something to do."

"It's kind of impressive, I suppose."

"Well then, thank you, I suppose."

"Don't do that in front of other people."

"Why not?" I said.

"Because a real octopus couldn't and that's what we're having you pretend to be. That means not talking to anyone else but me unless I say otherwise. And keep your third eye shut."

"Sounds like fun."

"It would've been before you betrayed me."

"Listen Nyx, I didn't betray you. I tried to tell you earlier but you wouldn't let me get a word in edgewise. Your parents really did throw themselves on me, weeping, trying to get my sympathy. I would've thrown them across the room, but I still don't know how strong I am in a waking world body. I thought if I broke them, you'd be mad at me."

Nyx suddenly shrunk in size. "Really? You don't like them better than me?"

"I don't like them at all. I'm not too fond of you right now either." I paused. I'd seen so many nightmares that could've been stopped if the person in had just spoken what they were thinking. "But I liked you last night. I've never liked anyone before."

Nyx brushed her pitch-black hair back behind one of her ears. "You're not just saying that?"

"What would be the point of lying?" I asked.

"Lots of people lie for lots of different reasons. My parents almost never tell the truth. They don't like me." Nyx's eyes stared at the grass by her feet and her voice suddenly became tiny. "No one does.

"There must be someone."

"You'll see when we get to school."

"So what's with all the color? Why do you dress so

differently for school?"

Nyx chuckled yet didn't seem very happy. "I don't. Wait and you'll see. Since we can't have you swinging like some sort of tentacled superhero, you'll have to ride on me. Preference between on my shoulder or on my backpack?"

I showed her my surprised face, which was basically everything on my head moved away from my eyes and mouth. "I get to choose?"

Nyx nodded and sighed. "Sure. You're not enslaved. You're just drafted. You can leave when my mission is done."

I reached a tentacle down to her backpack, kept one on the drainpipe, and lowered myself on her shoulder. Nyx smiled then touched my collar with the tip of a finger and whispered. "Away mode." There was a slight tingle. "You can leave the property now. Just don't get more than a couple of hundred feet away from me."

The girl in black walked out of the backyard, down the driveway to stop by the sidewalk. A couple of minutes later, a yellow school bus appeared at the corner. As it pulled closer, Nyx's pink outfit looked as if someone had poured ink on it as a wave of blackness stole away the neon pink color. By the time the wave faded, so had the unicorns and rainbows. They looked no different than the rest of the material, which was now an inky blackness so dark it seemed to absorb light.

"What just happened to your clothes?"

Nyx chuckled again and this one seemed to have some humor in it. "One of the side effects of me saving the world."

"In a video game?"

Nyx shook her head as the yellow school bus stopped in front of us.

21

Nyx puts her index finger over her lips. "As of right now, nobody else should hear you talk, got it?"

I nodded. Nyx grabbed hold of the rail with both hands and practically pulled herself up onto the bus as if her legs weren't up to the task alone. It took her quite some effort to reach the top step which is when the driver started screeching.

I guess the girl in black was as scary to her fellow humans as she was to me. It took me a moment to realize that Nyx wasn't who the driver was afraid of.

It was only when she pointed at me and began screaming even louder while trying to squirm backward out the tiny window beside her that I realized she was frightened of me.

I admit I puffed up a bit with pride. I hadn't even been trying and I had this woman terrified. "Sea monster! Get off the bus and kill it!"

I started to speak but saw Nyx glare sideways at me and shut up.

"It's not a sea monster, it's an octopus. And you can't kill it. It's my service and emotional support animal."

"No, it's not."

Nyx rolled her eyes. "You've heard of a service dog, haven't you?" The bus driver grabbed hold of her seatbelt strap and held it in front of her as if it was somehow going to ward me off, like I was a vampire and it was a cross. The woman nodded. "This is just like that. Only instead of a dog, my service animal is an octopus."

Nyx reached into her pocket and pulled out and unfolded

two sheets of paper. "This was a note from my doctor stating my diagnosis and my need for a service animal." That was signed by the father. "And this one is a letter from my attorney–" The mother. "– referencing the Americans With Disabilities Act as well as the laws governing service animals."

The bus driver wrinkled her brow frowned. "What does all that mean?"

"Legally, you have to allow my octopus Shivers on the bus."

"And if I don't?"

"You're opening yourself, the bus company, and the school district up for a multimillion-dollar lawsuit as well as to claims of discrimination."

The bus driver picked up the radio handle, then thought better of it. Instead, she dialed a number on her cell phone.

"Cecil, this is Marge. I got a kid here trying to get a service animal on the bus. No, not a dog. It's a freaking octopus. No, she don't have her phone out but hold on, I'll check."

The bus driver put her hand over the mouthpiece of the phone and turned the girl in black. "You ain't doing some internet prank, are you?"

Nyx shook her head. "Nope."

The bus driver grumbled. "No. I'm pretty sure she's serious. Well, she's got a letter from her doctor and lawyer and says she'll sue everybody if I don't let it on the bus. What I need to know is if I kick her off, will you and the company have my back? What do you mean am I sure it's an octopus? It's all squiggly with tentacles with the little sucker things on it. What do you mean I have to? No, I don't want to lose my job. Fine."

She smashed her finger down on the red button. "My boss is going to need a copy of those letters."

Nyx handed them over. "I figured. These are your copies

anyway."

The bus driver looked at both letters and folded them onto the dashboard.

"Is that thing well-trained?"

"Better than any other service animal in the world. Shivers, would you wave hi to the nice lady."

I leaned in and whispered in Nyx's ear. "Acting like a dumb animal is so far beneath me."

Nyx surprised me. I was expecting a command but was I got was, "Please?"

I relented, raised a single tentacle to wave back and forth.

This simple action seemed to amaze the driver. The woman must've had very low standards and expectations because this simple action appeared to amaze her. She stopped trying to squeeze away from me and waved back, then stuck her hand in the air between us.

"Shivers, shake the nice lady's hand."

Nyx couldn't be serious. Yet the expression on her face assured me she was.

I reached out my tentacle to touch her hand, careful not to let any of my suckers adhere to her skin. Our limbs moved up and down in sync then we let go.

The experience appeared to overwhelm the driver. Maybe she was an idiot.

"I guess maybe he is kinda cute." I take it back. She was obviously an intelligent woman with excellent taste. "Will he stay on your shoulder and not wander around the bus?"

Nyx nodded. "I'll make sure of it."

The woman motioned towards the back of the bus with a turn of her neck. "Get to your seat then."

"See that wasn't so bad. She thinks you're cute."

I'd always thought of myself as ruggedly handsome in a terrifying manner but could live with cute.

The other kids on the bus were staring our way as Nyx shuffled her way to find a seat. In that entire sea of teenaged faces, I couldn't spot a friendly one. As we walked down the aisle, kids who were sitting alone moved to the outside of the seat or slid their bags open over to make sure Nyx wouldn't sit next to them. She ended up taking the last empty seat.

I thought the ride would be uneventful, but I was about to learn that there were humans far meaner than nightmares.

22

A pair of heads popped up over the seatback behind us. The faces appeared to be pretty by human standards and the heads were covered with blond hair that came out of a bottle. While they both were smiling, their eyes held thinly veiled spite.

"Well if it isn't goth Nicki," said the blonde closest to the window.

"I thought she was emo. What's the difference?" said the blonde nearest the aisle.

"I don't know. They both wear black and act all depressed, so what difference does it make?"

"The name's Nyx, Connie."

"The name's Bonnie, you bloated waste of space. What's with the creepy-crawly? You know we stopped Show and Tell back in kindergarten, right?" said the blonde closest to the window, whose name was apparently Bonnie.

"Do you? You seem to always be telling about everybody else's faults as if it's some sort of a show," Nyx shot back.

"Well, with you we have enough nastiness to tell about for a whole season," said the blonde near the aisle.

"Good one, Tiffany," said Bonnie, giving the other blonde a fist bump.

"Yeah, that was so witty and funny, you should tweet it. That is if you can spell all the words," Nyx said.

"Moron. No one has to spell these days. Just tell your phone what to type and it does the spelling for you," Tiffany said.

"My bad. I forgot you didn't need to use your brain as long as you could use your phone."

"At least I'm not some fat, limpy loser who needs some stupid animal to be able to go to school," Tiffany said.

"Really? I thought that's what you had Bonnie for," Nyx said and held out a fist to me. It was a pretty good comeback, so I gave her a tentacle bump, which made both blondes squint in confusion.

"It understands English?" Bonnie said.

Nyx smiled. "Better than you."

Neither blonde had a comeback, so they simply disappeared behind the high back seat.

Nyx leaned in close. "Ignore them. A couple of privileged jerks who can't feel good about themselves unless they're making someone else miserable."

I leaned my head in so I was touching Nyx's ear. "Maybe they're related to the Nightmare King."

Nyx giggled.

At the corner, the bus stopped and a plastic bottle came over the top of the seat right towards Nyx, a blue drink pouring out on her head. I reached out with a tentacle and caught it in time to stop about a third of the bottle from pouring out, but I was too late for the rest. It had already covered the top of Nyx's head and was dripping down to her shoulders.

The two blond heads popped back up laughing.

"So sorry about that. We stopped so suddenly that I lost my grip," Bonnie said. The giggling stopped when they realized I was holding the bottle and there was still some liquid left.

I hadn't had breakfast, so I lifted the bottle to my mouth and drained what was left, then tossed the bottle back towards the blondes.

Bonnie had a white sweater with sleeves that were tied

around her neck. I reached up with a pair of tentacles, untied it, and brought it forward then used it to mop up the blue drink that was dripping from Nyx's head and clothes. It made some nice blotches on the snowy material.

"Hey! Your squid just stole my sweater!"

I kept rubbing the sweater to absorb as much of the drink as it could then reached back and tied the sweater back around her neck.

Bonnie squealed and squirmed, trying to get away from her own clothing.

"Ick. It's wet and sticky," she said as she pulled it off. "I'm going to send you my dry cleaning bill.

"Good luck getting Shivers to pay you. He is a service animal and was just taking care of the mess you made. If you don't sit back down and keep quiet until we get to school, I'll tell him to put your makeup on like you were clowns and we'll see what else he pulls out of your backpacks."

Bonnie and Tiffany both clutched their bags to their chest, horrified by the idea. I enjoyed envisioning using the makeup to give them a circus-style makeover. Or worse—to look like the Drooling Clown. Now there was a nightmare who knew how to scare.

Unfortunately for my fun, while they never shut up, they didn't bother Nyx for the rest of the bus ride.

23

Nyx had the power to control her parents, not to mention capture and give a nightmare physical form. Seeing a couple of mean girls treat her that way and Nyx letting them get away with it was messing with my mind.

I rode on her shoulder as we walked into what a sign said was Edgar Allan Poe High School. "Those twits are nothing special, right?"

Nyx rolled her eyes. "They certainly think they are."

"No, I mean they have no powers. They're just ordinary wakers."

"So? Most people are."

"But you aren't." Nyx was on a power level with no other human I've ever heard of. Sure, there were stories that the occasional sorcerer or witch could summon a nightmare and make it solid in the waking world for maybe a few hours at a time, but it wasn't easy for them. Making me real in her world hadn't put a strain on Nyx in any way I could tell. "You could destroy them with a single thought."

"Maybe a little more than that, but I try not to use magic for petty reasons."

"But why? You could rule this school. This town. Maybe even this world."

"That option *was* offered to me as an alternative to the jobs mentioned on career day."

Judging by her expression, she was being serious. "So why don't you? Why do you tolerate those girls' behavior towards you?"

Nyx shrugged. "Destruction is easy. Once I… someone

starts destroying, it's hard to stop. Besides, if I wiped out every person who was mean to me, this school would be almost empty. But my favorite reason is that not destroying everyone disappoints my parents."

"Your parents want you to destroy people?"

"You have no idea. They only had me because they wanted me to help extinguish most of the world. Luckily for the rest of the chumps here, I'm a rebel."

"You talk like you could destroy the world. That's ridiculous..." The dreaming and waking worlds were two sides of the same coin. If one ended, so would the other. "... isn't it?"

A great sadness seemed to invade Nyx's eyes and dim the twinkle that hid there.

I didn't get an answer, because a short boy who was skinny enough that a strong wind might've blown him over, ran over to us, screaming. I recognized him from the nightmare.

24

Having previously experienced a human screaming in my vicinity, this time I rightly assumed I was the cause.

There were some subtle differences between the two experiences. The first time the bus driver appeared terrified—a look I was both familiar and comfortable with. This guy was smiling and jumping up and down clapping. If I didn't know better–and I probably didn't–I'd say he was happy to see me.

"Oh my goodness, oh my gracious. Nyx, do you really have an octopus?" Irving asked.

I turned to see not only was Nyx smiling, but some of the twinkle had returned to her eyes. She glanced down and gave me a wink.

"Yes, Irving, I really have an octopus. He is both my service animal and my emotional support octopus. His name is Shivers."

Before I realized what was happening, the skinny kid's grubby little hands shot out and grabbed hold of me, his fingers weaving among my tentacles until he had a loose grip about where my collar was. Suddenly I was lifted into the air and found myself staring down into a pair of brown eyes through some very dirty glasses.

Irving twisted and flipped me over from side to side as he looked in all my nooks and crannies. I wasn't sure what had him so fascinated. Was he trying to figure out my gender? I would've been happy to tell him I was a male nightmare impersonating an octopus if he asked. Frankly, I don't think anyone outside of a marine biologist would know even how to tell if I was male or female.

The skinny teen let go of me with one hand and started stretching out my tentacles to examine them more closely.

I was trying to decide if I should slap him upside his head with a few tentacles or just simply grab hold of the nearby flagpole and snap myself away.

Before I could decide on either, Nyx swooped in, scooped me away from the manhandling beanpole, and put me back on her shoulder.

"Irving, you're not allowed to touch somebody's service animal while they're working."

"How can you tell if they're working?"

"They're wearing a vest."

"He doesn't have a vest."

Nyx facepalmed. "Excuse us for a minute."

"Not that you deserve this after being such a jerk, but I made something for you."

"What?" I asked suspiciously. The last thing she made for me was my shock collar.

Nyx held up an orange vest with nine small holes and one big one with the word *service animal* written on it.

"You can't seriously expect me to wear that?"

"Please?"

"I'll look ridiculous."

"You are a purple cephalopod nightmare. Why do you care how people think you look?"

"You have a point." I took it and held it up in front of me like it was a dead and stinky fish. "Does it do anything nasty like the collar?"

"Just a vest. And the collar is temporary."

"So you say. When did you make this?"

"When we were watching Princess Bride. You were so focused on the movie, you didn't notice."

"It was a great movie."

"It'll look great on you."

I sighed. I did like orange. "Fine. I'll try it on."

It fit me like an oddly shaped glove.

"Thank you," Nyx said.

We walked back over to Irving who had been staring at me the entire time. He couldn't hear us and apparently found nothing odd about Nyx acting like she was talking to an octopus.

"Shivers is so cool." Irving obviously had excellent taste. "Where can I get one?"

"Well first off, you need to have a medical diagnosis to justify getting a service animal."

A random girl walked by, apparently listening to the conversation. "I didn't know creepy was a medical diagnosis."

Nyx turned to scowl in her direction. The loudmouth girl wilted and scurried away.

"Oh, your rheumatoid arthritis," Irving said as we went inside the school.

Nyx nodded and I finally realized why she sometimes limped or seemed to have trouble with her hands.

"Second, Shivers is unique. As far as I know, he is the only service octopus in the world."

A weird noise came over the speakers in the hallway.

"That's the bell," Irving said. Not sure why they called it a bell. It wasn't ringing so much as giving off a buzz. "I've got to get to class. See you at lunch, Nyx."

"Bye, Irving," she said and started slowly down the hall.

I leaned in close to Nyx's ear. "I'm still trying to figure out exactly what a service animal is."

"Some people have special needs and animals can be

trained to help them. Dogs can help blind people get around or do things for people in wheelchairs. Heck, they can even sense seizures before they happen. There are some days I can barely move."

"So rheumatoid arthritis is your medical diagnosis?" I asked.

"One of them."

"How'd you dig the hole in your backyard then?"

"I didn't. I made my parents do it," Nyx said.

"You said one of them. What other ones do you have?"

"My father the doctor made sure that I got a phony diagnosis of schizophrenia when I was little which is a horrible thing for someone to have. I don't but my evil parents did a lot of horrible things to me that made it seem like I had many of the symptoms. It also allowed them to lock me away in a sanitarium or medicate me whenever I questioned or rebelled against them. But I do have PTSD."

"Why do you have posttraumatic stress disorder?"

"Mainly because some people tried to use me as a human sacrifice to end the world." I wanted more details but Nyx kept talking. "People with PTSD are allowed to have service animals for emotional support to allow them to function better around people. Despite being a bit of a jerk this morning at the house, having you with me *is* making me feel better and reducing my anxiety being in school especially with how you dealt with those twits on the bus, so thank you for that."

"Sure. You're welcome. Let's get back to this human sacrifice thing. Is that what was happening in your nightmare..."

Nyx placed her index finger over her lips as she approached the door that read *Girls Locker Room.*

"Too many people around to discuss the most traumatic day of my life. Right now, let's just get through with the most anxiety-producing class of my day."

25

The room we walked into was filled with rows of lockers. In between were a series of benches. A bunch of high school girls was changing out of whatever they were wearing into bright blue shorts and white T-shirts that read *Poe High School Physical Education*. Judging from the shirts, the school mascot was a raven.

Most of the students brought their own uniforms, but on the corner of one bench, there was a pair of blue shorts and a white T-shirt with a piece of paper on top with Nyx's name on it.

The other girls gave her a wide berth as she opened up her locker, took off her black clothes, and folded them neatly inside.

She quickly put on the shorts and shirt, picked me up from the bench to place me back on her shoulder, and practically ran out of the locker room. She didn't stop until a man—wearing the same uniform with the addition of a blue hat with PHS on it and a metal whistle hanging around his neck—stepped into her path.

The man, obviously the gym teacher, stood glaring at Nyx who slowed to a strut. As I looked down, the bright blue and white turned dingy as an inky darkness enveloped both the top and bottom until they were black.

"That's another gym uniform you've destroyed," yelled the man.

"I haven't destroyed it. It's right here," Nix countered.

"They're now defaced and don't match the rest of your class."

"This isn't exactly new, Coach Dere. You're well aware of my metabolic condition. My skin and sweat have a high level of acidity, which turns anything I wear black in a very short matter of time."

"That's bull crap! There's nothing anywhere on the net to back that up," the teacher shouted.

Nyx shrugged. "That's hardly my fault. And you've seen it happen dozens of times. Just let me wear the same one and no more uniforms need to be ruined," Nyx said.

"You'd like that, wouldn't you?"

"It would beat getting yelled at every stinking class, yes," Nyx said.

"Not gonna happen, little Miss Gothic Princess. It's got to be some sort of trick, a chemical, or something that you're using to change the color. I'll keep you doing it and one day you slip up and I'll find out your little trick and expose this as part of some twisted game."

"The only twisted game that's going to be happening here today is dodgeball," Nyx said.

Dere chuckled and puffed out his chest and part of his belly went with it.

"Bonus points to anyone who gets Miss Goth here out."

"Way to go in setting a good example by calling out a hit on a student," Nyx said.

"Prove it. Of course to do that you'd have to have a cell phone with you and according to the school handbook anyone who brings a cell phone to class gets a week's detention," said Coach Dere.

"Yes, you're an evil mastermind defeating my nefarious plots at every turn," Nyx said in a dull monotone.

Nyx turned to join the other students and the gym

teacher's pupils got wide. "What the hell is that thing? You know what, I don't care. There are no pets allowed in school. Get it out of here or that's an automatic week's detention for you."

Nyx smiled. "Nope."

"Did you just disobey a direct order from a teacher? Two weeks detention. March your goth butt down to the principal's office," Coach Dere screen.

"Double nope. Is it appropriate for you to be commenting on a student's butt?"

"In this class, I decide what's appropriate," Dere said.

"Maybe on your lunch break you should stop by the school library and grab one of the dictionaries. Then you can look up what the word appropriate means since you obviously have no clue."

"How about a month's detention and failing my class for the year?" Dere said.

"How about I name you in a million-dollar lawsuit for violating my rights under the Americans With Disabilities Act and you get suspended and then fired from your little job? Shivers here is a service animal which means what you just did broke the law. Ask me again so I can add another zero to the lawsuit," Nyx said.

"You ain't blind and that ain't no dog. Second, what kind of disability are you pretending to have?"

"You're not allowed to ask me about my medical conditions regarding a service animal. The only two legal questions are–is the animal a service animal required because of a disability and what work or task has the dog been trained to perform. You just keep adding more to the lawsuit."

"Try and prove it. These kids all hate you and if any of them go against my story, they fail my class, which means they get to go to summer school. You think anyone here cares enough about your fat butt to risk summer school to help you?"

"I wouldn't think of asking. I don't need to." Nyx pointed to her wrist. "I recorded our whole conversation on my smartwatch. Pretty sure the court will believe the recording."

"Thank you very much, Nyx. You just failed my class," Coach Dere said.

"Nope. The student handbook only lists cell phones. It makes no mention of any other recording devices. So how about we make a deal? You follow the law and pretend to act like you're a real teacher and maybe, just maybe, you'll still have a job in the morning."

Coach Dere came and towered over Nyx. She was only 5'5" and he was easily 6' 4". Dere appeared to expect her to be intimidated. He must have been very disappointed.

"Coach, your breath reeks. Here's a helpful hint-try to brush your teeth more than once a year."

Nyx hit the screen on the smartwatch and took a picture.

Dere reached down to try to grab hold of her wrist, but Nyx spun out of the way and kept clicking off pictures. The movement cost her—she was trying to hide a limp and only partly succeeding.

"Attempted assault on a student. That one adds jail time to the mix."

Dere got close enough to whisper, "It's bad enough that you stopped the ascension of the shadows, but you also made the Elders of the Temple of the Eternal Void disappear."

"A pity you weren't with the rest of the cult that night, but you didn't rank high enough. Would did you do for them again? Fetch the coffee? Or was that too difficult a task for you to manage?"

Dere addressed the class instead of Nyx. "New rules today. The sides are Nyx on one side and everyone else on the other. Anyone who hits the goth princess with a ball gets an automatic A for the semester." Dere opened up a closet on the side of the gym and rolled out a rack of basketballs then tossed them to the students who had spread out opposite where Nyx and I were standing.

"Coach, basketballs are a lot harder than dodgeballs. Won't someone get hurt?" a girl asked.

"I don't think anyone on your side has anything to worry about. Look at those flabby arms. Nyx will be lucky if she can reach any of you with a ball."

"Hey Coach," Nyx said, still hitting her watch. "Seems like everybody on the other side has a basketball but I don't have anything."

"You'll have your pick of balls in a minute." Most of the students weren't quite as bloodthirsty as the coach. Only a couple threw their balls which Nyx managed to dodge. The gym teacher noticed this.

"Anyone not making their best effort gets an F for the semester. Come on people, let's see those arms at work."

A ball came near Nyx and she slapped it with her hand. She then shook the hand like it hurt. "Oh darn. They got me. I'm out. They win."

Coach Dere shook his head. "Oh no, Nyx, that would hardly be fair to the other team. There are thirty-four of them and only one of you, so they'll have to get you thirty-four times before you're out."

The other side started throwing, some harder than others. There was one throwing harder than the rest. He was huge for a high school student. If he hadn't been recruited for the football team, the coach should lose his job.

Nyx was weaving and staying near the back, but her rheumatoid arthritis was getting worse—the more she moved the slower and stiffer she got. And the basketballs were coming closer and closer.

"Time to rearrange your creepy little face," said the behemoth as he threw his basketball, which missed Nyx's head by inches. He snatched another from a smaller boy's hands. This one launched like an intercontinental missile right toward Nyx's face.

The impact knocked her backward and she hit the floor so fast, I was thrown off.

I was a little disoriented and turned just in time to see the massive high schooler throw two more basketballs which smashed into me in rapid-fire succession.

I had never felt pain like this before. My dream body must not have had as many nerve endings. I did what I did when the King of Nightmares hit me—I let out a high-pitched wail and curled up into a ball.

"Shivers!" Nyx screamed, her face bloody.

I watched as the behemoth boy grabbed another pair of basketballs and threw them towards me.

I braced for impact.

26

It never came.

Nyx somehow leapt off the floor and launched herself across the gym to land in front of me like she was the star of a kung fu movie, then managed to catch a speeding basketball in each of her hands.

She stood there and bellowed in rage like a wounded animal. The room got darker as shadows filled her eyes and came out her nostrils, then flowed out from her fingers to envelop the pair of basketballs and turn them from orange to black in the same way I'd watched her clothes change, only this happened much faster and the inkiness was like a fire hose.

"Hey, Cole! No one hurts my friend!" Nyx yelled and launched the first black basketball back at the behemoth which nailed him in the groin. Behemoth fell to his knees with a high-pitched shriek of his own. Nyx didn't waste any time nailing him square in the face with the second black basketball. The impact snapped his head back as blood spurted from his nose. His body hung in the air for an instant before falling over backward unconscious.

Nyx put her foot on another basketball and flipped it onto the top of her foot and kicked it up so she caught it with both hands.

"Anybody else want a piece of this?" she yelled, her angry gaze sweeping her fellow students. Anyone holding a basketball dropped it and slowly backed off the now very dark court.

I closed my eyes for an instant and when they opened. Nyx was kneeling next to me and the room was bright again.

"Shivers, are you okay? Are you hurt?"

"This having a waking body is not all it's cracked up to be." I don't know how wakers dealt with this physical agony. I tried to wiggle everything. It seemed like all my tentacles still worked. "I think I'm hurt but not broken.

"I'm so sorry that happened," she said.

I had never gotten an apology before. "No need. It wasn't your fault. Why did you help me?"

"I take care of my friends."

"I guess you have at least one, huh?" I joked but was thrilled.

"At least two—you and Irving."

"But why? Especially after this morning?"

"Friends can argue and get mad at each other. That doesn't mean they're not friends."

"I wouldn't know. I never had a friend before."

"Well, I do whatever I can to make sure no one hurts my friends."

I felt a kind of warm sensation starting my center flew out through my tentacles. I liked it.

Coach Dere called Nyx some very unkind words that I was fairly certain teachers were not supposed to use in school, let alone hurl said words against a student. He was hunched over the behemoth whose eyes were still closed, but his chest was moving up and down.

"That wouldn't have happened if we used dodgeballs instead of basketballs," Nyx said with an edge in her voice.

Coach Dere's face was a deep red as he stood up and stomped towards the girl in black. "That's it. You are done at this school. You will be lucky if you don't end up in jail. I'm going to…"

The gym teacher stopped mid-rant and for good reason. The pair of basketballs that had been darkened by Nyx were now rolling under their own volition across the floor. When they got to Nyx, they rolled up her legs as if gravity had taken a holiday. I tried to fly. Sadly, gravity hadn't forgotten about me.

The dark basketballs kept going until they rolled out across her arms into her hands.

The coach's hand covered his mouth and he trembled. "You didn't stop the coming of the shadows. You are their fulfillment. You *are* the Queen of Darkness."

"Your Majesty will do," Nyx said in a sarcastic tone which was lost on the teacher who fell to his knees then bowed and groveled at her feet.

"Yes, Your Majesty. I am your humble servant and apologize for my transgressions against thee."

"Thee?" she said. "Who talks like that?"

The coach lifted his face from the floor with a confused. "Isn't that how one addresses the future ruler and destroyer of the world?"

"We're not in a Shakespearean drama. And I'm not going to destroy the world."

The gym teacher's look of confusion transformed into one of horror.

"At least not today."

Dere looked relieved. "Far be it from me, your humble servant, to question your mighty wisdom. What will you have me do?"

"First off, make sure that idiot gets medical attention. Second off, fix it so none of this affects me as it's your fault for having him attack me in the first place," Nyx said.

"Which I would've never done had I only known you

were the chosen of the shadows the Temple of the Eternal Void has been awaiting, Your Majesty. But I will make this go away for you. Should I kill *all* the students or just *one* to send a message to the rest of them not to talk to the principal or the authorities?"

Nyx sighed and her arms went limp by her sides as the basketballs fell to the floor, then rolled to snuggle against her ankles.

"No killing. No intimidation. And get up off your knees. The other kids are staring."

Coach Dere practically shot upright to a standing position. "Whatever you desire, Your Majesty. But I have to ask exactly how you expect me to make this go away by limiting my options like that?"

Nyx tilted her head back, so she was staring at the ceiling and let loose a grumble. She touched her nose as if she had just noticed it was swollen and bloody. "Never mind. Treat this like a normal teacher would."

Coach Dere's shoulders rose toward his ears as his face and his expression shifted to a mildly terrified one. "That means I would have to send you to the principal."

"Fine. I'll go to the principal."

Cole the behemoth moaned, shook his head, then sat up. His hand went to his face. "You broke my nose."

"Cole, get up and go to the school nurse," Coach Dere yelled then turned to Nyx as if looked for her approval. The girl in black ignored the teacher and walked toward the locker room.

I scurried after her.

27

After Nyx changed back to her regular black clothes, we headed to the principal's office. The two black basketballs followed, rolling behind us at a distance.

Nyx didn't seem to be bothered by it so I didn't mention it. The balls waited in the hall.

We sat in the main office for a few minutes until we were called into the principal's office. The man, dressed in a suit and tie, did not look happy. He motioned to the chair in front of his desk and Nyx sat.

"Nyx, I suppose you know why you're here."

"I have some idea, Dr. Sherman."

"I've been getting messages about you all day. All of it is the sort of thing that goes on your permanent record and can ruin your life. I was told your squid…"

"Octopus actually," Nyx corrected. I again refrained from pointing out that I was a tentacled night terror.

"Your octopus terrified your bus driver, assaulted two girls on the bus, and now I hear you assaulted Cole Hurston, the star running back of our football team."

"Only after he assaulted me and my octopus."

The principal sighed. "Yes, your octopus. I received your medical and legal documentation on your service octopus via email last night at home. And I did some research. I can find no evidence of an octopus having ever been used as a service animal before."

"You know me, sir. I'm an innovator."

"That is not the word any of your teachers would use, Nyx. Trust me. They've used plenty. So I have questions regarding your service animal."

"And being a high school principal with a doctorate in administration, not to mention access to Google, I expect it will just be a couple and they will be the right questions," Nyx said.

The principal seemed to be fighting the urge to roll his eyes. "Of course, is the animal in question a service animal for a disability?"

Nyx smiled. "Yes."

"And what services is the animal trained to provide?"

"Several. Besides providing emotional support, Shivers is able to assist with any task which my disability leaves me unable to perform, including but not limited to—opening doors, retrieving objects, and dialing 911."

The principal couldn't have had a more incredulous look on his face if Nyx told him she rode a unicorn to school that morning. "I find that last part very difficult to believe."

"Would you like to see a demonstration on a landline or cell phone?" Nyx said.

"You're serious?"

Nyx simply nodded.

"Fine, let's put an end to this farce. Use my desk phone."

"Shivers, call 911."

We had not gone over this, but I'd seen enough dream phones to know how they worked. With one tentacle, I lifted the receiver.

There was a sticker on the phone saying to dial 8 for an outside line, so I hit the 8 then 911 and watched as Dr. Sherman's jaw dropped.

A voice on the other end said, "911, what's your emergency?"

Dr. Sherman frantically grabbed at the receiver, pulling it out of my tentacled grip, and held it to his head. "No emergency, wrong number. So sorry."

Then he hung up the phone.

"So that is legitimately a service animal?" Nyx nodded. "This isn't a scam?" Nyx nodded again.

"I guess I'll send out an email to all the teachers and students to let them know. That is if I don't have to expel you for your assault on Cole. I've talked to his parents and they are furious."

"I'm sure they are. Can you imagine how ashamed the Hurstons must be over the fact that their gigantic son assaulted a girl over a foot shorter and a hundred pounds lighter than him? Not to mention also attacking a helpless service animal? What kind of beast have they raised?"

"But you weren't hurt," the principal said.

Nyx hadn't wiped the dried blood off her face. "I think my nose is broken, I hit the back of my head on the floor after he smashed me in the face. My entire body hurts. Do you know how sore something like this makes someone with rheumatoid arthritis? Plus, he hurt Shivers."

"The animal looks fine to me," Dr. Sherman said.

"I'm sorry. I had always assumed your Ph.D. was in administration, not marine biology. I never realized you were an expert on octopuses. My mistake."

The principal stammered. "Well, not an expert. And the correct term is octopi."

"No, it's not. It would be if it came from Latin, but it comes from Greek so it is octopuses."

I liked octopi better but doubted I got a vote.

The principal typed into his laptop. "Hmm. It seems you are right. You learn something new every day."

"Exactly, like your expertise on octopuses. So just looking

at him, you must be able to tell see how injured he is."

Nyx turned to me, so the principal couldn't see her face as she gave me a wink. I stumbled across the desk, moving my tentacles as if they hurt.

"Now I have to find a vet who specializes in marine life. We may have to travel hundreds of miles. What if it is so bad, Shivers can't keep working? Do you know how much this kind of service animal costs?"

"I have no idea." The principal typed into his laptop and his face turned pale. "It says here a typical service animal can run thirty thousand dollars."

"For a *dog*. Remember, this is the first service *octopus* in the world and its costs include research and development. I imagine his cost was fifty to a hundred times that of a dog."

"That's at least a million and a half to three million dollars," Dr. Sherman whispered.

"Aren't government grants amazing? Since this attack happened on school grounds during a school-sanctioned activity, that means the school will be on the hook for repaying that amount to his trainers, shared with Cole's family of course. Plus, the expense of buying me a new service octopus. So, if Cole's parents want to play chicken with this, fine. Let's rev up our engines cause I ain't swerving. Poe High School has a zero-tolerance policy, which means you have to suspend or expel both of us. I'm a freshman but he's a senior. He received a full football scholarship to an Ivy League college, didn't he? I remember you posing next to him for the picture in the paper."

The principal nodded.

"Suspension for assaulting a tiny freshman girl with rheumatoid arthritis and her service animal would certainly mess up his chances of keeping that scholarship, especially if this matter goes viral on social media. If we are both expelled,

I imagine his scholarship disappears entirely. Not only will his family be out the cost of an Ivy League education, but they'll be responsible for the money for his injuries to Shivers. And the shame on their family name. Not to mention my pain and suffering, which is significant. I'll probably have to start seeing a shrink three or four times a week for years."

The principal started tapping his hand nervously on the table. "Maybe we should get your parents in here first."

"Sure, we could do that but there's a reason you haven't already called them and we both know it. Once my mother hears about this, it will only be a matter of hours before that lawsuit gets filed against Cole. And since he is only seventeen, his family too. And of course, the school. And I'm sure you and the teacher will be named as well. The only way my mother doesn't sue everybody is if she never hears about it. It's your call, Dr. Sherman. Do we suspend or expel both of us and makes a big case out of this or-" Nyx smiled. "-sweep this under the rug?"

"Nyx, I don't think you realize how serious this is. You assaulted another student to the point he lost consciousness."

"Dr. Sherman, do you think I enjoy repeating myself? The stress of sitting in here is flaring up my RA. I acted in self-defense of myself and my animal. You know what? I'm done dealing with you. Let's just call the police and let them sort it out. Oh, I may have forgotten to mention I have audio and pictures of what happened."

The principal slammed his hand on his desk.

"Trying to threaten me? I can slam stuff too." Nyx picked up a book and hit the desk with it. Her glare made her eyes darken and the principal slid his wheeled chair back, away from her. "Shivers, call 911."

Dr. Sherman reached out and pulled the desk phone to his chest and pulled out the wire from the wall. "I already interviewed some of the other students in the class and their versions of what happened coincide with yours."

"Excellent. My mother will insist on depositions from all those students as will the police, I'm sure. Instead of having my father look at my nose, I demand to be taken to the emergency room," Nyx said.

"Well…" interjected the principal but Nyx was on a roll. There was no way he was getting a word in until she let him.

"We will need to know why in a school-sanctioned gym class, all the students were put in danger by replacing softer dodgeballs with hard basketballs in a game banned by many school districts across the country because of its inherent violence and risk of injury. Then all the students were instructed to assault a single student with a known disability. I can only imagine where social media and the local news channels will run with that information. Some of the other students may claim emotional trauma from being forced to attack a fellow student and sue the school district as well. I can imagine thirty some odd lawsuits won't look good on *your* permanent record, Dr. Sherman."

"Young lady, I don't respond well to threats."

"I guess it's a good thing for you I haven't made any. I've only stated the obvious. If you feel threatened by the truth, that's hardly my fault, is it?"

The principal tapped his hands on his desk rapidly. "There is also the matter of you destroying school uniforms by dying them all black. Destruction of school property is also a suspendable offense."

"So having a medical condition that causes clothes to turn black is now suspendable? That's a civil rights violation there. Lucky for me I can easily prove my condition in front of a jury or television cameras. I already told you, I'm not swerving. So, what's it going to be? Are you calling my mother and the cops, then kicking me and Cole out of school or are you turning out of my fricking path, making me free to go back to class?"

The principal leaned over and glared. "You can go back to class, Nyx, but no one can keep pulling stunts like you do and get away with it forever. Screwup once and it will be my great pleasure to expel you from school."

Nyx got up and walked to the office door. "It's good for you to have goals. Have a wonderful day, Dr. Sherman."

28

When we exited into the main office, Cole Hurston was sitting in a chair. He was so big he had to pick one without armrests so he could fit. His nose was taped and he had an ice pack on his groin.

When he saw Nyx, he stood up to block her way.

"You took a cheap shot, freak. I'm going to find you when nobody is around and pound your goth ass into black jelly."

"As big as you are, maybe you shouldn't call anyone else a freak. And I look forward to nobody else being around because I won't have to hold back. You have no clue who you're dealing with."

As if in answer to Nyx's words, the office door smashed open and the two black basketballs rolled in.

The behemoth turned. "What the @#%?"

Oddly no one else in the room turned to look. Instead, they all seemed to become very intent and focused on whatever else they were doing.

"A big man threatening a little girl. Although pretty much everyone else is small compared to you around here which is why you have terrorized those around you for years. You hurt me and you hurt my friend Shivers."

Cole laughed. "You're such a freak that your only friend isn't even human."

"Shivers is still smarter than you, Coley. I'm putting you on notice—your days of hurting others are over and done. My little friends are going to be following you around from now on."

Cole squinted. "Your octopus?"

"Nope." Nyx pointed at the black basketballs. "Them."

Cole slapped his knee and let out a loud, mocking laugh. "If you think I'm supposed to be scared because you put wires or some robotics club crap on a couple of basketballs so they roll on their own, you have no idea who you are dealing with."

Nyx looked down at the balls and nodded, seeming to tell them what to do without saying a word.

One ball bounced up and hit Cole under the chin and the second in his chest. The one-two combination knocked him to the ground. The secretary looked over, saw the balls and her face went blank and she turned back to whatever she had been doing on her computer.

Cole rolled over onto all fours, attempting to stand back up and the ball did another double bounce, this time onto his back, flattening him to the ground.

Nyx went down on a knee next to Cole's head. "I'm not joking. From today on, they will know if you try to hurt or are even mean to someone. Whatever you do to someone else, they will do worse to you. Touch me or one of my friends again, and you will never hurt anyone ever again. Do we have an understanding?"

"@#% you..." Cole cursed but the black basketballs bounced rapidly on either side of his head, smashing into the floor so hard the tiles were cracking. "Yes! We have an understanding."

"Good. They say people have the chance to be anything they want, so if nothing else, I will make sure that you will want to be kind."

Nyx strutted out of the office.

29

"Nyx, that was some hard-core nightmare level stuff back there," I said. "What's going on with the basketballs? Are they alive? Have you ever done anything like that before?" I asked.

Nyx shook her head. "No. I normally have to hold back my power, but I guess was so angry I must have stopped restraining myself and the power just flowed out. I'm not sure how they became sentient or if they are alive or not, but they can feel my emotions and are drawn to protect me."

"That's the same power that leaks out and turns your clothes black?" Nyx nodded. "Maybe one day or your laundry will come to life, too." What a nightmare that would be—someone getting attacked by dirty socks and underwear.

"That would certainly make doing laundry much more interesting. And letting loose that power got rid of all the pain that normally makes my whole body hurt. I only got rheumatoid arthritis after I got this power. I can't remember ever feeling this good, even before. I think it even fixed my broken nose."

"How come no one seems to notice the black basketballs moving around?" I said.

"The power comes from the Void, a place of such utter darkness that one unfiltered glance at the manifestation of shadow from that abyss dimension would terrorize and probably paralyze most people. The human mind has a safety mechanism that makes people ignore its shadows so they don't collapse sobbing into a mess of mad human flesh.

"And that dark power is inside of you?"

Nyx nodded. "Some of it."

"Why aren't you driven mad?"

"Not sure. I had to face the source to survive so maybe that victory gives me some protection."

"Can other humans sense what's in you?"

"Sadly, yep. I try to keep it bottled up inside, but it's not a perfect seal. It leaks."

"Like when it turned your clothing black."

"Yes."

"Since it's not as much as you used on the basketballs, it's not enough to make them ignore you."

"Uh-huh. And humans sense that the darkness inside me is their primordial enemy. That hate and fear it."

"Which is why so many people dislike you."

"Pretty much."

"But not everyone. Irving likes you. Why doesn't it affect him?"

"Irving has some magic of his own. Not a lot, but it lets him see the core of who a person is. It lets him look past the darkness to see the real me."

"But Irving seemed to like me," he said.

"He did. So?"

"All the other people I met here and in the dream realm are afraid of me, but if Irving can see what's inside, and he likes me then that means–"

"That you're really good?" Nyx smiled. "I already told you that."

"Yeah, you did." The idea was a shock but in a good way. The Nightmare King was wrong. I'm not a worthless waste of space.

"Why doesn't the darkness affect me like the humans?" I asked.

"The way I figure it, you've always lived in a place filled with nightmares and terror, so the idea of darkness doesn't affect you the same as a human who has lived in relative safety their whole lives."

"So that's why you've been alone."

"Mostly." Nyx gave me a sad smile. "But mostly is still better than entirely. And thanks to you, I am far less lonely than I was."

Nyx held up a fist. I bumped her back with a balled-up tentacle.

"Me too."

30

I rode into the cafeteria on Nyx's shoulder. She stepped into a line and picked up a plastic tray. In front of us, there was a metal counter with clear plastic shields that showed an assortment of things with steam rising off them.

I leaned in close to Nyx's ear and whispered, "What is that stuff?"

"Food," she whispered back.

I thought she was kidding, but I watched as the things got scooped onto trays and given to students.

"It doesn't look as good as the stuff we had at your house."

"It isn't, but it's not that bad. What do you want me to get for you?"

So many choices and none of them appealing. "What are the yellow tubes?"

"Fish sticks."

"That I guess," I whispered.

"Two orders of fish sticks, please," Nyx said.

One on the other side of the counter a woman with her hair up in a bun scowled. "You have to pay for the second order. No freebies."

"I'm aware. Extra tartar sauce, please."

Nyx got baby carrot sticks and ranch, a banana, and a bag of chips. A woman at the end of the line sat behind a cash register, hit some buttons, and motioned with her head for Nyx to keep moving, not bothering to exchange any pleasantries. She had gushed over the three previous students.

The girl in black walked past crowds of kids congregated at other tables and kept going until she reached one in the far back, away from most everyone else. She plopped her tray down and sat.

I climbed down from Nyx's shoulder onto the table. She used a plastic fork to separate the fish sticks into two equal piles. "Help yourself."

Tentatively, I wrapped a tentacle around a yellow tube and plucked it from my pile. I dangled it in front of my face. The yellow coloring seemed to come from breading of some sort. The stuff beneath that looked white.

I brought it to my mouth and used my beak to bite off a chunk.

It wasn't bad.

"Try dipping it in the tartar sauce," Nyx suggested.

I did which improved the taste. As I was dunking the last third back into the tartar sauce, Irving sat down across from us.

"Nyx, I don't think your octopus is supposed to eat fish sticks. Octopuses eat things like crab, fish, sea stars, and even occasionally other octopuses," Irving said.

"Someone is suddenly well versed in Marine biology," Nyx said.

"I looked it up on Google."

Irving looked over at me and his eyes made a circle of all my tentacles.

"Also Shivers has nine tentacles. An octopus has eight. It's right there in the name. Octo is Greek for eight."

Nyx shrugged. "Shivers has a rare mutation and he is very sensitive about it."

Irving nodded as if this made perfect sense. "Did you also know that all octopuses are venomous to different degrees if they bite somebody with their beak?"

Nyx nodded. "I did."

She did? I didn't know that. Was *I* venomous?

As if he could read my mind, Irving asked, "Is Shivers venomous?"

"Very, but he knows not to bite anyone."

Well, I hadn't been planning on biting anyone but now I kind of wanted to just to see what happened. Not that I would. Dream injuries go away on waking. Real-world ones, not so much. Besides, humans look like they'd taste awful, especially the teenagers.

I picked up the fish stick and rolled the entire thing in the tartar sauce and put it in my mouth whole.

"Aren't you going to stop him? Shivers might get sick," Irving said.

Nyx peeled a banana, broke it in two, and offered half to me. I reached out took it.

"Shivers will be fine."

As I put the half banana in my mouth, Irving frowned. "I didn't see anything online about an octopus being able to eat berries."

"A banana is a fruit," Nyx said.

"True, but it's classified as a berry but all berries are fruit, so I guess either one is technically correct." Irving stared at me as if he was waiting for me to start convulsing or throwing up. I thought about doing either, but as Irving could see the real me. I figured I try to be as good as possible. "Also an octopus had 3 stomachs and nine brains, a regular one and a small one for each tentacle. With nine tentacles, I guess Shivers must have ten."

Irving turned to chat with the girl in black about their classes and other boring waker school-related things.

When my fish sticks were gone, Nyx poured baby carrots onto the same spot on the tray. They were hard and crunchy.

I dipped the second one in the tartar sauce.

"Ick," Nyx said and tore open a white packet and squeezed white liquid onto the tray.

"Try this. Carrots taste better with ranch."

She was right.

Irving glanced at his phone. "I've got to go to my band lesson." He looked over his shoulder. When I followed his gaze, I saw the three wakers from the nightmare Nyx had me create. "Maybe they won't notice me leaving."

"Or maybe today will be the last day they ever bother you," Nyx said.

Irving rolled his eyes. "Yeah, right. And after that, I'll get elected homecoming king and get a recording contract as the world's first tuba hip hop artist. Wish me luck." Irving got up, dumped his tray in a garbage can, stuck it on a ledge in a window, then snuck out a side door.

"I did better than that," Nyx said and winked at me.

31

Irving would never make it as a ninja. No sooner had he got through the cafeteria door than the three guys from the nightmare stood and rushed out a different door.

Nyx held out her hand towards me and I climbed on her shoulder. "We're up."

Nyx rushed across the cafeteria, pausing to dump the remains of our lunch into a garbage can then toss our tray into the window. We hurried through the same door Irving had.

"Exactly what are we up to?"

Nyx turned towards me with a confused expression. "I thought you understood what was going on."

"Explain it to me like I didn't."

"Those three have been beating up Irving. Using my darkness on them would be way too harsh, maybe even deadly, which is why I recruited you to give them that shared nightmare last night. Now we're going to use your powers to give them a follow-up nightmare in the waking world that's so scary they will never even consider bothering Irving again."

"Wait a second. I can create nightmares in the waking world?"

Nyx nodded. "Thanks to that collar I developed you can. It focuses your power."

"Not even the Nightmare King can do that."

"He can. It just upsets the balance of things if he does it too often."

"Won't me doing it upset this balance?"

"Nope. You're not as powerful as him and I'm lending you a bit of power. This waking nightmare should barely be a blip on the mystic radar. Somebody would have to be looking for it at the same time you did it to even notice."

"So how do I do it?"

"I figure pretty much the same way you would in the dreaming."

"You figure?" I said. "You don't know?"

Nyx shrugged. "It's not like I've done this before. I'm mostly just winging it."

I was not filled with confidence.

We rushed to catch up. "So when they hit Irving, he feels pain like I did earlier?"

Nyx nodded. "That plus feelings of shame and embarrassment for not being strong enough to defend himself so it crushes his ego and destroys his self-worth."

"And you'd rather do this than call your black basketballs? I mean if you can do that, you didn't exactly need to get me involved."

"When I put this in motion, I didn't know I could do that and I'm really in favor of minimizing violence. Cole is all about violence and if I didn't do something, he would have pounded me—and probably you—after school. Of course, if this doesn't work, I suppose that's always an option."

We caught up to Irving just as the bullies three surrounded him in the same hallway that I had re-created in the nightmare.

"Give us your lunch money," said Chuck.

"You know I can't do that. Our parents put money on our accounts with credit cards. And even if I paid with cash, I already ate lunch so I would've already spent it," Irving pointed out as if the bully was an idiot for not seeing what he thought was obvious.

"Fine, give us your allowance," Steve said.

"I don't get one."

"Then tomorrow bring us a hundred bucks," John said.

"And a chocolate cake," added Chuck.

"I'm not going to do either of those things," Irving said.

"Then you leave us no choice. We have to beat you up today and again tomorrow," Steve said.

"You might not be so lucky this time. I've been watching MeTube videos on self-defense." Irving said brought his fists up in front of his body as if he was a martial arts expert who'd gotten confused on how fighting actually worked.

The three bullies shook with laughter. Chuck shoved Irving into the wall.

"I'll tell the principal."

"Go ahead," Steve said. "There are no cameras on this hall so it'll be your word against ours and we outnumber you."

"I noticed," Irving said.

"Who do you think they'll believe?"

"Me probably," Nyx said and the bullies three startled and turned to face her. "Step aside, meatheads."

Nyx plowed in between the bullies standing in front of Irving. She opened the door.

"Irving, go to your tuba lesson. I'll take care of this. They won't bother you again."

"Ooo. Little Irving needs his girlfriend to fight his battles for him," John teased.

Both Nyx's and Irving's cheeks turn red.

"She's not my girlfriend," Irving said in a tone twinged with both embarrassment and regret. "I mean she's my friend and she's a girl. And she's awesome but…"

Nyx was so flustered she was momentarily speechless, but she gently put a hand on Irving's shoulder and herded him through the door before he could say any more.

Nyx spun around to face the bullies, her hands on her hips.

"Don't think we won't hit you because you're a girl, freakazoid. We're all about equal rights," Steve said.

"Fine by me. That means I get to hit you back, just like I did Cole in gym class."

"That didn't happen or they would've kicked you out of school," said John.

"What the heck is that thing on your shoulder?" Chuck demanded.

That's when Nyx stole my line and said, "Your worst nightmare."

32

It was the perfect cue, so I focused on creating a nightmare.

And nothing happened. Nyx turned her head to look at me and I shrugged my tentacles.

Chuck chuckled. "It'll take a lot more than some uncooked calamari to scare me." To accentuate his point, the bully took his finger and poked me between my two front eyes.

The shock made anger bubble up inside of me and the nightmare exploded around us.

Nyx transformed into a waking dream version of Irving who slammed back through the doors and started growing and didn't stop until he smashed through the ceiling to tower over us. Not that the physical world was harmed—we had just shifted slightly out of phase with the waking reality.

Giant dream Irving's fingers transformed into tentacles that plucked Steve, John, and Chuck off the floor and into the dream sky—which was filled with a thunderstorm.

The tentacles rose higher until the bullies three dangled upside-down over Dream Irving's giant mouth which was filled with tentacles and chainsaw teeth.

Chuck screeched, flapping his arm as if trying to swim away. "Please don't eat us. We'll never bother you again!"

"We won't even come near you!" John promised, pushing against the tentacle he was wrapped in.

"We'll do anything you want!" Steve pleaded, just hugging himself as his head swung back and forth over the giant mouth. "Just let us go!"

"Hmm," said Dream Irving, the tentacle fingers of his other hand stroking his chin.

"Here's what you are going to do then. Tomorrow, you are going to give me a hundred dollars. Each. And make me a chocolate cake."

"Sure, we'll have the cash," Steve said.

"We're really good bakers," Chuck promised.

"We are?" John said. Still upside-down Chuck reached out and punched him in his gut.

"Shut up!" Chuck whispered. "Of course we are. If we're not, why would he let us go if he thought we were going to make him bad cake?"

John upside-down nodded and rubbed his battered stomach. "We're really great bakers! We're totally always making stuff for bake sales."

"And if I let you go, none of you will ever bully anyone again. And you will not tell anybody that this happened or next time I'm not going to let you go. I will eat you instead so I can save my lunch money that day. Don't even mention this to me. I'm going to pretend that it never happened. I suggest you three do the same. Think you can handle that?"

"Yes sir," Chuck said.

"Absolutely," Steve agreed. "You've made us see the error of our ways."

"Consider it handled," John promised.

Nyx's giant version of Irving lowered the three bullies to the floor, then bent over so the face and the mouth of terror stared down on the unkind trio.

"Run away!"

They did.

❝❞

"**I**t worked!" Nyx said with equal parts happiness and surprise.

"Think they'll leave Irving alone now?" I asked.

"They believe he can turn into a giant monster so it's safe to assume they won't risk bothering him again."

I held up my tentacle. "And if they don't, we'll have to teach them the same lesson over and over until it sticks."

Nyx smiled and fist-bumped my tentacle.

From inside the band room came a funky tuba beat.

Nyx started moving around like she was convulsing.

"Are you having a seizure something?" I said.

"No, I'm engaging in the practice commonly known as a happy dance."

"You're a horrible dancer," I teased.

"People should sing and dance whenever they want to whether they're good at it or not. I suppose you think you can do better," Nyx challenged.

"With eight tentacles tied behind my back." I stood up what some might consider my two leg tentacles, my moves quickly putting any human dancer to shame.

"Not bad, Shivers." Nyx stood next to me and did the best she could to imitate my moves with her limited number of limbs.

"That's an improvement at least," I said.

Nyx held out a hand towards me. I placed a tentacle in her palm and stretched my tentacles that were on the floor so

I rose until we were the same height. She twirled me then I returned the favor. Nyx swung me in a circle, so I grabbed the front of her shoulders and did the same. Next, we stood next to each other and did a kick line, her with one leg at a time, and four tentacles alternating for me. As we did this, a teacher rounded the corner. He was tall, thin, and balding and wore wireframe glasses. He slowed to stare at us. We froze until the teacher walked past, although he paused to look back before turning the next corner. Once he left, we danced our way back to the cafeteria.

34

At the end of the day, the bus dropped us back at her driveway. I waved to the driver. She smiled and waved back before driving off.

"It seems you're likable enough that you cancel out my scariness," Nyx said.

"As good-looking as I am, would you expect anything less?"

Nyx smiled. "That was the best day I've had in high school that I can remember, all because of you. Thanks. Would you consider staying on with me?"

"Huh? I didn't think I had a choice."

"I needed your help to make sure those three bullies wouldn't bother Irving. We did that. Your obligation to me is paid. You can do anything you want." Nyx opened the door and stepped inside.

If I was free, that meant that Nyx was telling the truth. And if that's the case, that meant her parents were lying.

Oh, figments. Her parents! The candles! In all the fun and excitement, I totally forgot.

"Nyx, I have to tell you something!"

The father stepped out from behind the door, grabbed Nyx around the head and neck, and held a cloth over her face.

"Hush little terror. You will not ruin our surprise," said the mother as she poured a potion on me and I passed out.

35

would say I woke, but I wasn't asleep. My mind was just frozen.

I was in a very familiar feeling basement. Chains ran from my collar to the wall.

Nyx was chained to a picnic table.

It goes without saying that I had a bad feeling about this.

"Nyx! Wake up!"

Nyx's whole body twitched and her eyes opened and she turned her head to look around.

"Not again!"

This had happened to her before? Then it hit me why I recognized this place. The was the real-world place where her nightmare happened, where the robed people were chanting and trying to stab her with the dark knife.

"How did my parents get free of the binding spell?"

I cleared my throat. "I may know something about that."

A door opened on the far side of the room.

"You should. After all, you did it," said the mother strutting into the room. The father followed. Both wore black robes just like in Nyx's nightmare, although instead of a knife, they carried piles of her darkened laundry which they dumped near a wall.

"Shivers wouldn't do that," Nyx said.

"I'm afraid he did, daughter," said.

"Shivers, is that true?" Nyx asked.

"It is, but I'm sorry. They told me you were lying, that I

was enslaved. Then after the way you treated me this morning, I thought they were telling the truth. They said if I blew out the binding candles, they take off my collar and I'd be free. I was wrong. I'm so sorry."

"My parents tried to kill me to open up a portal to the dark realm so ancient darkness could destroy the world. Now they are trying again."

"Daughter, you were always such a drama queen. That's not our intention at all," said the father.

"So you're not trying to summon creatures from the dark realm to destroy the world?" I asked.

"Oh no, we're going to do that," the mother said. "We're just not going to have to kill our daughter this time around."

"So you did try to kill Nyx?" I asked.

"Oh yes. After all, that's what the Temple of the Eternal Void is all about," said the father. "We just had to wait for certain stars to align for *that* sacrifice and summoning to work."

"It was the only reason we had a child," the mother said. "I mean really, having to push her out of my body and then feed her, change her diapers, and take care of her for all these years. Who would want to be bothered? Motherhood has truly been the worst experience of my life, but we needed a sacrifice. Turns out that several of the Temple worshippers who had children for the cause grew attached to their spawn. When the time came, they didn't want to kill them to open the way for the majestic darkness to come to this world," the mother said.

"They got so whiny about it. 'Please spare my child! Blah, blah, blah,'" the father mocked. "They lacked true devotion to the cause."

"That they did," the mother agreed. "Fortunately, we weren't plagued by such pathetic weakness. On the unfortunate side, our ungrateful brat went and ruined the ceremony."

"How?" I asked.

"I hijacked the spell," Nyx said.

"Which is something no normal fourteen-year-old girl should be able to do," the mother said.

"She was sneaky and looked at our most sacred book and somehow was able to read the language. I minored in ancient languages before I went to med school. It took me years to learn enough to read the dark texts," the father said.

"Not my fault you didn't think to use Google Translate," Nyx said.

"To start the summoning, I sliced her palms and the bottoms of her feet—you need blood to get these a good summoning rolling—as my husband chanted the spell. This little shrew starts chanting faster and in English, no less, so when the portal opened, she controlled it instead of us," mother said.

"There wasn't a whole lot of control to be had. I just make sure I had some and you didn't have any."

"The blood in the spell was enough to open the portal a little bit," the mother said. "I was going to stab this bane of our existence through the heart in order to open the portal wide enough to grant a dusker, one of the great dark ones, entry into our world."

"Just one?" I asked.

"We figured we'd start with one rather than a screaming horde of thousands, so it'd be easier to control," the father said.

"Then this harpy hit her own mother like the nasty child she is."

"You were about to stab me in my heart. I think a punch in the nose was more than justified," Nyx said.

"If you were chained down, how do you reach?" I said.

"I dislocated my thumb. I saw how to do it in a movie. It

was excruciating, but it was better than being stabbed. Plus, the manacles were made for an adult so I had a little wiggle room," Nyx said as she pulled against her chains.

"We fixed that issue this time around," the father said.

"Then after she punched me, this ungrateful brat grabbed the knife out of my hands like a lousy little thief," the mother said.

"And she didn't even have the sense to use it to stab us to save herself," the father said. "She just threw it away like the little wimpy baby that she is."

"I didn't want to stab my parents even though they were trying to kill me. Considering the position I'm in at the moment, I'm willing to concede that compassion and mercy were both character flaws and a huge mistake," Nyx said.

"That didn't stop you from killing the rest of the Elders of the Temple of the Eternal Void," the father said.

"I didn't exactly have control over the dusker when its dark tendrils reached into our world and dragged the rest of the cult members into the darkness and their deaths."

"Each death made the portal bigger," the father said. "Then the little thief stole more than a knife. She stole the power that was destined to be mine!"

"A cascade of black energy came through the rift and disintegrated my chains to dust before lifting me and filling me with dark and ancient power," Nyx said.

"She became the Queen of Darkness instead of me," the father whined.

"Shouldn't you have been the King of Darkness?" I said.

"That's not how the ancients wrote the title in the book. For the kind of power it offered, they could call me the pretty princess of shifting shadows and I wouldn't care because I would become the channel for the dark void and through it, control the world," the father said.

"That's all nice and good," Nyx said. "But those stars won't be in alignment again for three hundred and sixty-seven years, so you won't get another chance to summon a dusker."

"We don't need the stars anymore because part of the dark realm is already here on Earth," the mother said. "Inside you. It's been leaking out onto your clothes, so with a bit of blood and your dirty laundry, we can bring a dusker over," the mother said.

"You won't be able to control it. You still won't be the Queen of Darkness, so what does that get you?" Nyx said.

"You chose to save humanity and vanquish the dark ones. We will offer them a chance at revenge by killing you and as a reward, they will make me the new Queen of Darkness," the father said.

"But you said you weren't going to kill Nyx," I said.

"Weren't you paying attention? *We're* not going to kill her. A dark one is," the mother said.

"You'll never be able to control the power, let alone a dusker," Nyx said.

"You dare tell me I can't control the power when it's you who is too weak! Too weak in mind, body, and spirit. Given enough time, the darkness will eat away your body. It has already started devouring your joints, given you rheumatoid arthritis. And fool that you are, you endure that agony rather than letting the darkness out and using it. If you did that, your bodies' torment would end and you would have no more pain."

"And people would die," Nyx said.

"Bah," said the father. "People die all the time. What does it matter so long as their deaths bring you power over those who are left? I have learned from your weakness. I'll use the power as it was intended–to subjugate humankind and control the world."

"You are ignoring your own prophecies. The dark queen is mentioned for a reason. The power will not work for you," Nyx said.

"No worries. Then we'll just go with Plan B," the mother said.

"Plan B?" The father's head tilted in confusion. "We don't have a Plan B."

"You may not, dear." The mother reach into her sleeve and pulled out a folded piece of cloth and shoved it over her husband's face and held it there. A short time later, his eyes rolled back and he fell to the floor. "But I do."

36

From her other sleeve, the mother told a syringe with a long needle. "I took this from your father's work."

"Doesn't that make you a little thief too?" Nyx said with extreme sarcasm.

"It's only office supplies. Employers budget losing a percentage to employee pilfering."

The mother placed the needle in the crook of Nyx's left elbow and pulled the plunger back, filling the syringe with the crimson blood of the girl in black.

"Mom, you really don't want to do this."

"Oh, how sweet. You finally called me 'Mom' again. Not that it matters, because I *so* want to do this."

The mother walked up to a music stand with an open book on it.

"I wish I'd known about the Google Translate thing. I had to secretly record your father practicing the chant and learn to say it phonetically. Your way would've been so much easier."

Holding the syringe over the black clothes, the mother pressed gently on the plunger. A single drop of blood fell onto the laundry. There was a flash of light and a release of black mist where it made contact.

The mother took out a piece of paper, placed it on the book, and chanted, pausing every few seconds to squirt more blood on the pile of laundry.

Nyx was squirming and doing her best to pull free of the chains but her best wasn't good enough.

Nyx turned her head towards me and shouted, "*Shivers be unbound!*"

My collar fell off.

"Shivers, get out of here. Go back to the Dream Realm. At least you'll be safe."

"Why are you freeing me? This is all my fault."

"My parents tricked me for my entire life. I can't blame you for being fooled once, especially after I was a jerk to you. I don't want my friend to get hurt. Go!"

She didn't have to tell me thrice. I skittered along the floor to the door which the parents never bothered to close after they came in.

Instead of racing off like I wanted to, I stopped on the other side of the door and looked back.

Nyx still struggled helplessly at her chains. She was going to die if somebody didn't do something. The only somebody around was me.

A bad dream would run away, only thinking of themselves. But I had learned something about the real me during my time with Nyx.

I wasn't bad.

Grabbing hold of either side of the doorway with a tentacle, I walked myself back. With a jump, I shot forward, soaring through the air and landing next to Nyx on the picnic table.

"Turn the chains black like you did the basketballs."

Nyx shook her head. "I'm trying, but it's not working. They must have coated them with a spell. Get out of here before she notices you're free."

"I'm not leaving my friend behind."

Bracing myself with my two leg tentacles, I wrapped the other seven around the chain that connected to her right wrist. I pulled and pulled. Then I pulled some more. Then

I think I pulled a few muscles. The chain held fast, but the wood of the picnic table bent. I gave up pulling on the metal and focused instead on the wood.

I tore the board in half so the piece the chain was bolted to dangled.

I repeated the process three more times.

Nyx was free but looked like an old-fashioned ghost in chains like Jacob Marley from a Christmas Carol.

She rolled off the table, the chains falling behind her.

"Come on, let's get out of here," I said.

Nyx shook her head. "If my mother gains control of that much power, she's going to hurt and kill a lot of people."

"Maybe, but if we get out of here now, you and I won't be two of them," I said.

The girl in black shook her head. "I have to stop her."

"Why? Especially the way the people around here treat you."

"Because I'm the only one who can."

Nyx ran at her mother and knocked her to the ground in a crappy tackle, but it was enough to make the book fall free. Sadly, the woman didn't stop speaking. Nyx tried to cover her mouth to shut her up, but the mother just chomped down and bit the girl in black's fingers.

"You're too late, daughter. Soon the power you squandered will be mine. You can't stop me."

"We'll see about that," Nyx said, but the impact of her words was lessened as a portal to primordial darkness opened on the wall.

37

Misty darkness seeped from the portal and oozed its way right towards Nyx. Although it didn't seem solid, it latched onto her ankle and flipped her upside down to dangle helplessly.

"Mother, don't do this! Please! The darkness feels nothing but hatred towards all life. Even one dusker will kill millions, maybe more."

"That's your problem, daughter. You think too small which is why you're such an underachiever. With me in charge, the death toll will be *billions*. That'll still leave plenty of survivors whose only purpose will be to serve me."

"But it won't be you. The darkness will eventually take you over, and control you, body and soul," Nyx said.

"My will is far too strong for that to happen." The mother pulled herself up.

"Hello darkness, my dear friend," the mother shouted dramatically as if she was on a stage. "I open this portal to the Void with the blood of the Queen of Darkness mixed with your dark essence. As a sacrifice to your greatness, I offer my own daughter, she who stole your power and used it to banish you. Let her blood and death nourish the purity of your darkness and allow one of you to cross into my world where you will rule as a god. All I ask in exchange is for you to transfer your gifts from this ungrateful wretch to me, your most faithful and loving servant, so that I might faithfully execute your bidding and bring forth bring a new age of shadow and death upon this horrid world. I…"

The inky tendrils stopped swinging Nyx like a pendulum, perhaps considering the mother's evil offer.

Before there was an answer, the mother's eyes rolled back, she went limp, and fell to the floor.

Behind where she had stood was the father, holding the leather-bound book of dark magic he had just used to smash his wife's head in.

"Dark Ones, I offer you a far better sacrifice than this miserable pretender. Not only do I offer you my own flesh and blood in the form of my daughter, but also my wife who foolishly believed herself to be my equal. You can feast upon the life light of them both in exchange for making me, your ever-faithful servant, the new Queen of Shadows.

"Father, don't!" Nyx shouted, still dangling upside down. "The darkness will devour all that you are. You will never be able to control the power!"

The father laughed. "Daughter, if you have controlled and contained the dark essence of the Void this long, I will no have difficulty whatsoever."

Nyx wiggled and squirmed against the shadowy tendrils that held her ankles, giving her all to make it let go of her. The darkness was not impressed as the chains and bits of picnic table on her legs swung to smack the sides of the girl in black. The ones on her arms dangled above the floor.

"You have always been a narcissistic, egotistical idiot," Nyx said. "I suppose I couldn't expect you suddenly develop common sense or do the right thing."

"Nor could I," said the mother, jumping up from the floor to grab hold of the leather book. She yanked back with all her body weight, but the father didn't let go.

"Don't be a fool! Show some sense woman and submit to your husband's will. Out of all those who live on this world,

I am only one truly worthy of being the Queen of Shadows."

The mother pointed with her chin to where I was cowering beneath the picnic table. "Even that pitiful nightmare creature knows it should be me."

"Don't bring me into it. I didn't ask to be part of this. I don't even want to be here," I said.

"Then leave. My pitiful daughter has already freed you from her control. There is no reason for you to stay," the mother said.

"I'm not leaving without Nyx," I said.

"Then you won't be leaving at all," the father said. "I will just add you to my sacrifice."

A tremendous bang on the other side of the dark portal shook the room.

"ENOUGH!" boomed a voice as dark as the deepest night. "WHICHEVER OF YOU SPILLS THE QUEEN OF SHADOW'S LIFEBLOOD WHILE I HOLD HER SHALL BECOME OUR NEW VESSEL."

The parents both grinned as if the thought of killing their daughter made them the happiest they've ever been in all of their miserable existence.

The mother was closest. When she let go of the book, she picked up her dark blade and stepped toward Nyx.

I slingshotted myself across the room and aimed for her face. I landed perfectly and wrapped my tentacles about her head.

The mother smashed the hilt of the knife into her forehead. Pain shot through me but the mother's blow had hurt her too, probably more than it did me, at least judging by her muffled screams beneath me. The mother clawed at my body, trying to get me off her face. Humans couldn't hold their breath long, so I held on, hoping she'd passed out.

Realizing what I was doing, she turned the knife so the

tip was inches from one of my tentacles.

When she jabbed, I let go of her face to scurry onto her back. Her arm swung around so the blade followed in an attempt to stab me. The mother had enough finesse that she didn't cut herself.

Now that she could breathe she decided to ignore me and spun back toward Nyx.

It was time to find out if I was venomous.

Slithering over to her side, I crossed under her armpit and clamped my beak down below the robe sleeve onto her forearm.

It took a few seconds, but her body stiffened then froze like a statue. Keeping a watchful eye on the knife still in her hand, I scurried around to her stomach. I reached up and waved a tentacle in front of her face. There were a few twitches of her eyeballs, but otherwise, she didn't move any more than a statue.

Meanwhile, the father was trying to put a rag over the girl in black's face while she dangled upside down from the moving bits of darkness, but Nyx was hitting him with her arms, the chains, and wooden bits of picnic table. She even bit him. Sadly, Nyx wasn't venomous, so he didn't do much other than yank his arm away. I looked for something to latch my tentacles around so I could slingshot onto the father when I heard a familiar, rhythmic thumping.

It grew louder.

The two black basketballs dribbled themselves down the steps then rocketed through the open door into the basement. Each hit a wall and ricocheted into the father, one hitting his knee from the side with a sickening pop and the other smashing his jaw. As the horrible parental figure crumpled to the floor, I sling-shotted my way to him, grabbing the chemical-soaked rag from his hand. With a tentacle, I held it over his mouth and nose until he passed out.

From the other side of the portal came a sound that was equal parts growl and thunder.

Tendrils of shadow were no longer satisfied holding only Nyx's ankles. They took her wrists and throat then twisted her in the air like a toddler punishing a doll.

"YOU ARE THE MOST DISAPPOINTING HUMAN OF ALL TIME. YOUR WORLD SHOULD BE DEVOID OF LIGHT, WITH HORDES OF HUMAN HUSKS SERVING OUR GREAT DARKNESS."

"I don't want to destroy the world," Nyx shouted. "Go back where you came from and leave humanity alone!"

"YET YOU ACCEPTED THE GIFTS OF DARKNESS WHICH EVEN NOW FLOW THROUGH YOUR BONES AND VEINS."

"Yes, I hijacked the summoning spell because I didn't want to die. It was the only way to send you back to the Void. I became Queen of Shadows so you couldn't kill me and everyone else on Earth."

"NOT EVERYONE. WE WILL NEED SLAVES TO SERVE US. MAKE GOOD ON YOUR SACRED OBLIGATION AND LEAD OUR DARK CHARGE AGAINST THE LIGHT OF THIS MISERABLE ORB. ACT LIKE THE QUEEN OF DARKNESS SHOULD."

"Not interested."

A small tendril slithered its way into Nyx's nostril, seeming to reach deep inside her head.

The darkness made noises as if searching through Nyx's mind.

"WHY ARE YOU NOT? FEW HUMANS TREAT YOU WITH ANYTHING BUT SCORN. HOLDING OUR COSMIC DARKNESS BACK, TRAPPING IT IN YOUR BODY AS YOU HAVE BEEN DOES NOTHING BUT CAUSE YOU SUFFERING AND ANGUISH AS IT EATS AWAY AT YOU FROM THE INSIDE OUT. RELEASING OUR SHADOW WILL SOOTHE YOUR PAIN. IN TIME, IT WILL

BRING YOU PLEASURE AND SATISFACTION LIKE YOU HAVE NEVER KNOWN. THE MORE YOU USE, THE BETTER IT WILL FEEL. YOU NEED NEVER FEEL AGONY IN BODY OR SPIRIT EVER AGAIN. WE DO NOT HAVE TO KILL ALL HUMANS. YOU CAN MAKE THOSE WHO HAVE TREATED YOU WITH CRUELTY AND DISRESPECT INTO YOUR SLAVES. WOULD THAT NOT BE FAR BETTER THAN HAVING TO ENDURE THEIR TORMENT?"

Nyx struggled for breath when darkness suddenly flared from her eyes, reaching out and tearing the tendril from her nose.

"Get out of my mind!"

The darkness on the other side of the portal thundered again. The vibrations shook the house down to its foundation.

"YES. THAT IS IT. LET THE ETERNAL SHADOWS FLOW FROM THE VOID THROUGH YOU AND DO YOUR BIDDING. WE ASK NOTHING MORE THAN FOR YOU TO PUNISH THOSE WHO DESERVE IT BECAUSE THEY HURT YOU. THE MORE SHADOW YOU BRING FORTH, THE MORE INFLUENCE OUR DARKNESS WILL HAVE UPON THIS WORLD FILLED WITH THE SICKENING LIFE LIGHT. ONCE YOU HAVE BROUGHT FORTH ENOUGH SHADOW, THE WALL BETWEEN OUR REALMS WILL FALL. AFTER AN ETERNITY OF BANISHMENT, WE SHALL RETURN AND DEVOUR THE ABERRANCE THAT IS LIFE."

"Get used to disappointment because I'm not letting you out." The darkness in Nyx's eyes reached out further and grabbed hold of the inky tendrils restraining her wrists while the black basketballs bounced and pummeled the darkness that bound her ankles.

An instant later, the girl in black was free, but she didn't fall. Her own shadows held her aloft as she spun to face the portal to the dark realm. The chains fell off her.

"USING DARKNESS AGAINST DARKNESS IS A FOOLISH

WASTE OF POWER. WE SHOULD JUST EXTINGUISH YOUR LIFE LIGHT AND TAKE OUR GIFT BACK TO BESTOW ON A MORE SUBSERVIENT HUMAN. OR PERHAPS WE WILL ALLOW YOU TO KEEP ON FIGHTING UNTIL YOU HAVE BROUGHT FORTH ENOUGH SHADOW THAT THE WALLS FALL, THEN INSTEAD OF A REWARD, YOU WILL BE PUNISHED THROUGHOUT ETERNITY. DOES FIGHTING US SEEM WISE NOW?"

"I'm open to a peaceful resolution but I doubt you're going to take your shadows and go home. If you want to kill humanity, you're going to have to go through me to do it."

"SO BE IT."

Misty darkness poured out of the portal right at Nyx, ready to kill her.

That is until some idiot jumped in front of it.

38

In case you hadn't guessed it, that idiot was me.

Standing on two stretched tentacles, I sprang between Nyx and the portal. I slapped away the tendrils reaching for the girl in black with my free tentacles, which was about as effective as standing in front of an open fire hydrant and trying to block the water by swinging a spoon.

"A nightmare existing outside of the Dream Realm is just another bit of life light to extinguish."

The darkness grabbed hold of my tentacles and pulled me like I was taffy.

The writhing inky blackness stretched me until my solid body tore and ripped. In seconds I would be shredded into nine tentacles and a head. My struggles availed my not a bit as I might as well have been trying to pull down a skyscraper.

Fear came at me hard and I did something I had seen untold humans do when confronted with a nightmare.

I panicked.

Deep inside me from a part of my soul I didn't know existed, my first feeling of absolute terror rose up, dragging with it something that I had done thousands of times. My dream creating power surged out a thousand times more powerful than ever before, blasting out from my three eyes and mouth into the dark portal to envelop what was on the other side.

I summoned the granddaddy of all nightmares. I knew instantly it hadn't come from either of the parents or even

Nyx. This wasn't a human nightmare. I was tapping into the terrors of the creatures of eternal shadow from the far side of the Void.

What does utter and total evil darkness fear? The question made my entire body shiver in horror and anticipation of the answer.

The answer was terrible to contemplate, yet I didn't stop creating the nightmare.

I'd never done anything like this. I'd only brought nightmares to people. I trembled with the strain of creating the nightmare of the ultimate darkness. If I played a part in the terror to come, I might lose control and the dream would vanish. Someone else needed to play the part of whatever terror came forth.

The only being I trusted in the universe was here.

"Nyx, I need you to do what you did when we linked the bullies three." I didn't want to give away exactly what I was doing as if the duskers knew, it probably wouldn't work.

The girl in black's pupils got wide when she realized I was transforming reality into a dream but she nodded in understanding.

The nightmare grew around us, but nothing was changing. Nyx stayed Nyx, not transforming into whatever horror would terrify the primordial shadows.

A glow enveloped Nyx. The darkness pouring out of her eyes was replaced by light.

The girl in black was no more. Nyx the light burned bright and pure, bleaching her dark clothes pure white, then did the same to her hair.

A noise that sounds like a storm cloud stuffed full of explosions that had learned to scream in pain boomed from the other side of the portal.

The darkness shrieked, **"NOOOO!"**

The brilliance pouring out of the teenage girl intensified, causing the darkness on both sides of the portal to whither and smoke. The inky tendrils near me shifted away to focus on Nyx. The glowing girl grew in response, both in size and intensity.

Nyx became so luminous I had to squint to look at her.

That was when I realized what the darkness feared—the life light inside of humans, particularly Nyx.

Resplendent beams shot out of her hands, blasting the dark tendrils aside. The misty darkness shriveled, decaying to dust under the assault of Nyx's light.

The home of darkness sent enough shadows through the portal to swallow a football field but they couldn't dim Nyx. When they enveloped her, Nyx transformed into a teenager-sized sun. The otherworldly darkness pounded and gnawed at Nyx, but this dream was my creation. I was in charge of how things worked here. Screw stupid physics. Time to show these dusker scum how we rolled in the Dream Realm. Nyx floated higher and held her hands out to her side to form a sphere of light in front of her stomach. It grew until it dwarfed her body. Now she as so bright that I couldn't look near her, not even squinting with my third eye.

"Shivers, throw the laundry with the blood into the portal! Make sure you get all of it!" Nyx screamed

Careful not to lose focus, I slithered over and in rapid-fire sequence, flung every last bit of clothing into the dark realm.

"I stand between you and humanity. If any dusker tries to harm my world again, I will destroy you all!"

To accentuate her point, Nyx brought her arms in front of her until her wrist met with her palms. The pure white sphere exploded and flaking light burst from her hands into the portal. The tendrils of darkness on our side convulsed as the thundering shrieks from the Void grew to almost disintegrate the cement under our feet. All the oozing darkness fled back through the portal from whence it came.

"THIS IS NOT OVER, CHILD. YOU SHALL NOT LIVE FOREVER. WE HAVE WAITED BILLIONS OF YEARS TO RETURN. WHAT MATTERS A FEW MORE? THROUGH YOU, OUR DARKNESS REMAINS IN YOUR WORLD. ONE DAY YOU SHALL YET CHOOSE TO USE IT AS WE INTENDED. DO IT OFTEN ENOUGH AND THE WALLS BETWEEN REALMS SHALL FALL AND NO AMOUNT OF LIGHT WILL STOP US FROM EXTINGUISHING THE LIFE LIGHTS OF ALL HUMANITY."

The booming became so loud I thought the house would shake into rubble but before the structure could be destroyed, the portal vanished as if it had never been there at all.

The darkness had run away from Nyx and slammed the door closed behind them.

39

With the portal closed, the source of my nightmare was gone so it ended. Nyx was back to being the girl in black.

"They're gone!" I said. "You beat it!"

"No, *we* beat it." Nyx turned back to look at her parents. The mother was still frozen in place, her pupils so large they had swallowed her irises. The father had woken and was curled into the fetal position, whimpering.

"Our next dilemma is what do we do with the scum who gave birth to me?"

"You should've thrown them through the portal," I said.

"I considered it." The father's whimpers intensified and he put his thumb in his mouth to suck on like a baby. Nyx sighed. "But as I keep saying, *I've* never killed anybody. Besides, I can't think of anything that would be worse for them than having to behave as if they're good people and do everything I say."

"I'm sorry about having blown out the candles," I said.

"Shivers, you just saved my life and together we saved the entire world. I can forgive one mistake." The girl in black scary glared at me. "But just one."

"I appreciate that."

"Would you be so kind as to run up to my room and bring down those two black candles?"

"Sure Nyx, but are you going to be okay with them until I get back?"

"Mother appears to still be frozen. Which leads me to my next question—why is she frozen?"

I beamed. "It turns out, I *am* venomous."

Nyx smiled. "Good for you. And if Father dares move out of the position he's in, there is a lot I can do to him that will leave him alive but wishing he wasn't."

The black basketballs moved to either side of the father and bounced menacingly within inches of his head and groin. The father whimpered a bit more then squeezed his legs tighter to his chest and sucked so hard, he practically swallowed his thumb.

I stretched my tentacles so that I reached the door with one step and the top of the stairs with a second.

It wasn't long at all before I returned with the pair of wax tubes. Nyx pulled the dark blade from her mother's immobile hand, carefully opening her fingers. With the knife, she pricked the mother's index finger and dipped the wick of one candle into the blood that pooled there then repeated the process with the father.

She uttered a few words I couldn't quite understand and both wicks burst into flame.

"Mother, you can move again. Father, get on your feet. We're going back to the old rules as of now. To reiterate, you must obey me in all things. You can do nothing whatsoever that will harm me in any way, directly or indirectly." She spent several minutes listing forbidden activities. "You will behave as good people would." Another long list of forbidden activities. "You are unable to enter my bedroom or room. And there is a new rule—neither of you will do anything that will in any way harm Shivers."

"Yes daughter," the evil parents responded in unison.

"Now go upstairs and make us dinner. I'm in the mood for pizza. How about you, Shivers?"

"Pizza sounds good to me."

40

The pizza was good. After we finished, the parents did the dishes.

"Now both of you go to bed now," Nyx ordered.

"But it's not even seven o'clock," the mother whined.

The girl back in black shrugged.

"May we have something to eat first?" the father asked.

"No," Nyx said.

"Just a little bite of the leftover pizza?" pleaded the mother.

"I'd be happy to bite both of you," I said.

The father's pupils grew three sizes and the mother's skin became very pale.

Nyx stroked her chin. "Another time, Shivers. Now both of you go."

Slouching and bowing their head, the parents said in unison, "Yes daughter."

"And no TV, phones, or reading!" the girl in black shouted at their backs.

Their grumbling made Nyx smile.

Considering they had tried to murder her a second time, they were getting off easy.

There was enough leftover confections in the freezer that we made ourselves a couple of ice cream sundaes. This time, I ate slow and avoided the headache.

"That nightmare you created was impressive," Nyx said.

"Thanks. I couldn't have done it without the power you gave me," I said.

"Shivers, the power I gave you was in the collar which had fallen off you. That wasn't me. That was all you."

"That's not possible. I doubt the Nightmare King could've done that on his own, let alone someone like me."

"Yet you did it. Maybe the Nightmare King has some competition to worry about."

My mind was having trouble wrapping itself around the implications, so I just stared into space for a long time.

"That was a good scenario for your nightmare," Nyx finally said.

"It wasn't mine," I said.

"It certainly wasn't mine. One of my parents?" Nyx said.

"Nope." I smiled. "I tapped into the minds of the dark ones."

"I couldn't see the thing I turned into this time. What were they were afraid of?"

"You."

"The thing the eternal darkness fears the most is… me?"

I nodded. "You are pretty scary."

"They think I have that much light inside of me?" Nyx said.

"Apparently."

"Whoa." It was Nyx's turn to stare off into space for a bit.

I made and finished a second sundae, then asked, "So what happens now?"

"That's up to you, I guess. You're free to do whatever you want. Although if you want to stay in the waking world, you will have to wear the collar."

"Wait a second. You said I was free so why do I have to wear the collar?"

"I will remove all the containment and punishment spells but the magic I stored in the collar is what lets you have a solid form in the waking world. Without it, you will turn insubstantial within a day, maybe two."

"And automatically be sucked back into the dreaming."

Nyx nodded. "There's enough magic in the collar for you to stay solid for at least a century."

"In the dreaming, I'd live for thousands of years but out here, only a century?" I asked.

The girl in black shrugged. "I'm not sure but I don't see why not. With the collar, you can go anywhere on Earth and do whatever you like. Or take it off and go back to dreaming when you fade."

"If I decide to stay in the waking world, do you want me to go off exploring?"

"I want you to do what will make you happy," Nyx said.

Remembering all the nightmares that were caused by poor communication, I said, "I appreciate that. What would make *you* happy?"

"I'd like you to stay here and live with me. When my rheumatoid arthritis flares up, it's hard to do basic things so I really could use your help with day-to-day stuff too."

"So you need me to be your service *animal*? An emotional support nightmare?"

"Sure, I *need* that but what I *want* is for my friend to stay with me and not go away."

"Am I really your friend?" I whispered.

"You have to ask?" Nyx said.

"With everything I've been through in my existence, I do."

"You're really my friend. My best friend in fact. Am I really *your* friend?"

I turned her words back on her. "Do you really need to ask?"

Nyx smiled and opened up her arms. "No, I don't."

Nyx wrapped her arms around me and I returned the

favor with my tentacles and I had my first ever real hug.

"What are you going to do?" Nyx asked as we separated.

"I've never had a friend or a home before. I very much want both. I'm staying." Although I wondered if the Nightmare King had noticed that I was missing. And what was he going to do when he does realize it?

"My parents may be evil scumbags but they're right about one thing," Nyx said.

"What's that?"

"You are a good hugger."

41

It wasn't quite as odd watching Nyx going to sleep for the second time. She climbed into her bed, fluffed her pillows five times, then lay down on her side, and pulled the covers up to her chin.

"Good night, Shivers."

"Good night, Nyx."

"See you in the morning."

"You bet," I said, not looking forward to being bored again.

I took a spot on the ceiling and watched as Nyx closed her eyes.

Unlike the first time, her body didn't relax and her breathing didn't slow.

Her body tensed and Nyx pulled the covers over her head. Her body started to shake and there was sobbing beneath the blankets.

Like a spider moving from ceiling to bed, I lowered myself down on a single tentacle until I dangled in front of the girl in black's covered face.

"Nyx, are you okay?"

She responded by pretending to snore.

"Nyx, I know you aren't sleeping." I peeled the covers off to reveal her tear-covered face. "Why are you crying?"

"Sometimes things overwhelm me. Everyone hates me. I saved the world from being devoured by darkness. Twice. Which means every jerk at school is only alive because of me.

There is something inside of me that wants to kill them all and the only thing stopping it from getting what it wants is me. What thanks do I get? Shadows eating my body slowly from the inside out and getting treated like crap by almost every person I meet. Nobody knows or cares about what I did. Or about me with two exceptions. The people who are supposed to protect and love me have tried to kill me twice. My life sucks. It gets to me sometimes."

"That does suck," I agreed.

Nyx gave me a sad little chuckle. "You suck at cheering someone up."

"I've never had to try before."

I wasn't even sure I knew how. But I've felt the same way she did with far less reason. So I asked myself, *What would have helped me?*

"Nyx, you are the scariest human I have ever met."

"Thanks," Nyx said. I recognized the sarcasm in her tone.

"I'm a nightmare. That is a huge compliment. You are brave and tough. You could have run away from the portal to the Void. I even told you to, but you didn't. Instead, you risked your life to save everyone, knowing full well that people wouldn't thank you but that didn't enter into your thinking. You also saved Irving from those three bullies without him knowing. Does it really matter what other people think?"

"A little. And it would be nice to be thanked."

I nodded. "Nyx, on behalf of all the mean and stupid humans, and more importantly one very handsome nightmare, thank you for saving the world."

Nyx sniffled and wiped her tears and nose drippings onto the corner of her sheet. "You're welcome."

"And I don't let people hurt my friends, so there's that," I said.

"Is that so?" Nyx said.

I nodded. "Yep. It's something my best friend taught me."

There was more eye wiping. "She sounds pretty wonderful."

"She is."

"Go to sleep, Nyx. I'll be here when you wake up."

"Are you sure?"

"I'm not going anywhere."

Nyx held out her hand and I wrapped my tentacle around it. Nyx gently squeezed it and closed her eyes.

It wasn't long before she was asleep.

And as I settled in on her nightstand holding onto my best friend's hand, I wasn't bored.

42

The next morning, we got on the school bus. I waved at the driver. She smiled and waved back.

As we walked down the aisle, we got the same dirty looks followed by the shifting of seats and bags but Nyx stood taller than she had yesterday, barely seeming to notice.

Again, the only open seat was in front of the blond twits.

"Hello, goth Nicki," Bonnie said.

"Buzz off, Connie," Nyx said.

The pair said some more mean things which Nyx ignored. Not only were they mean twits, apparently the blondes lacked any creativity because when we got to the same stop sign, a sports drink bottle came over the seat in the upside-down position. The only difference was today the drink was purple instead of blue.

Well, not the only difference but the others were all on our part. Nyx had been expecting it and was recording it on her phone as my tentacle snatched the drink out of Bonnie's hand and turned it so half its contents poured on top of Bonnie and the other half on Tiffany. I quickly followed that with two other tentacles drawing clown-like smiles and eyebrows on both girls' faces with twin lipsticks we'd taken from Nyx's mother's purse. Nyx had vetoed making them look like the Drooling Clown after my description. She felt it was far too disturbing.

As soon as my tentacles were out of the way, Nyx snapped some pictures of the mean clown girls.

"I must say both of you ladies are looking particularly lovely today." Nyx turned the screen so they could see the picture. "Wouldn't you agree?"

Tiffany tried to pluck the camera out of Nyx's arthritic fingers, but I snapped my tentacle like a whip onto her wrist. The mean blonde yanked her hand away.

"You better delete that," Bonnie said.

"That is if you know what's good for you," Tiffany said.

Nyx fiddled with the screen. "No, I don't think I will. I saved it to the cloud. I must admit, I'm sorely tempted to post it. Of course, that's just a screenshot from the video I took which I think will make a lovely post, don't you?"

"You wouldn't dare!" Tiffany whined.

"Think that if it makes you feel better." Nyx turned to me and smiled. "You know what, I think I'll hold off for the moment. But the next time I hear something nasty come out of your mouths or if something sticky or wet is thrown on me by you or your friends, I will make sure I post that."

"Are you blackmailing us?" Tiffany said.

"I wouldn't consider it blackmail. I'm simply agreeing not to embarrass you if you stop being mean to me. Blackmail would be is if I also added a payment plan to that."

Other people on the bus had taken notice of the mean blondes and were laughing at their makeup. Phones were coming out and the twits noticed.

The blondes pulled their coats over their faces and scrubbed the makeup off their faces, after which they started to work on fixing their sticky hair.

They ignored us for the rest of the ride. I was disappointed that they got all the lipstick off their faces.

In gym class, an already darkened pair of shorts and a T-shirt awaited us in the girls' locker room. When Nyx walked out, Coach Dere was waiting, but not to give Nyx grief. Instead, he stood and bowed at the waist and whispered, "Welcome to my humble Phys Ed class, Your Majesty."

After the portal had closed, the dark basketballs had snuggled against Nyx and then bounced their way out of the house again. They were positioned on either side of Cole who looked bruised and battered.

The jock rushed over to us. Following the gym teacher's lead, he bowed at the waist to the girl in black.

"Nyx, you have to help me. I went to football practice yesterday and every time I tackled somebody, your basketballs beat me up. You have to fix it so I can play. If I can't, I'll lose my scholarship."

"Are your parents dropping the complaints and any lawsuits against me?"

"Oh yes. I talked to them and Dr. Sherman and convinced them to let everything go."

Nyx held her arms up and the black basketballs bounced into her hands. She pulled them in for a hug, planting a kiss on top of each of them.

"How are my babies today?" Nyx paused as if they were answering her. Maybe they were.

She appreciated them coming to help her last night. They had sensed she was in danger then came of their own accord to help and it had endeared them to the girl in black. Besides, I guess she was technically their mother, or at least their creator.

"I'm glad to hear that. I'm very proud of both of you. I think that perhaps Cole is starting to learn his lesson so let him play football without any punishment."

Cole put both his hands together, then straightened and bent his elbows while bowing his head. "Thank you so much, Nyx."

"Unless he breaks the rules and hurts somebody."

Cole's face went pale. "Oh no, I would never do that. I've learned my lesson. I'm a changed man."

"I certainly hope so but it's going to take a lot for me to believe it. Perhaps if you started going out of your way to help other people instead of hurting them? That might show that you've grown and changed."

Cole nodded his head. "You're right. I should do more community service. What type of work should I do?"

"That's up to you to decide. I'd recommend something that you find fulfilling."

Coach Dere waited until Nyx was done talking to Cole before he called the class to order. Oddly, he was the only one besides Cole who seemed to notice the sentient basketballs. Everyone else's subconscious seemed to be working very hard to ignore their existence.

Nobody got hit with a ball.

43

At lunchtime, we were sitting at the same table in the back with Irving, who was thoughtful enough to have bought a ring of frozen shrimp for me that were just about defrosted. The shrimp were good but far better with the cocktail sauce. Nyx had suggested I peel the skin and get rid of the tails but found I liked them better with the crunchy bits attached.

Irving and Nyx took turns throwing shrimp to me as I plucked them out of the air with my beak and mouth. It was fun and tasty.

"At least I don't have a tuba lesson today, so I don't have to worry about those three bullies," Irving said.

"I'm telling you, you won't have to worry about them anymore," the girl in black said.

"Nyx, I can't see any reason why they'd suddenly stop," Irving said, then looked behind me. "Oh no."

I swiveled my head a hundred and eighty degrees and saw Steve, John, and Chuck walking towards our table with their hands behind their backs. I turned back around and Irving looked like he was going to bolt. He still had a shrimp in his hand. I hoped he'd be courteous enough to throw it to me before he ran away.

Nyx laid a calming hand on his shoulder. "Relax. They're not going to do anything."

"Why? Because of the cameras in the cafeteria?" Irving said.

"That too," Nyx said.

Steve was at the center of the approaching triangle.

"Irving, we want to again say we are so sorry for yesterday and all the other days we picked on you. We're very sorry and I want to again assure you it won't happen anymore."

"Again?" Irving said.

Nyx her index finger over her lips. "Shush. Just hear them out."

"As promised, we have chocolate cake," John said, pulling the confection from behind his back. Steve and Chuck did the same. "Unfortunately, due to poor planning on our part, we made you three cakes instead of one. We hope this is okay."

Irving squinted looked around as if he was waiting for someone to jump out and say it was a prank. "Sure, that's fine. I love chocolate cake."

"So you're pleased?" Chuck asked.

"Yeah, sure," Irving said.

"So you don't have a problem with us," Steve said.

"Um…"

"Irving does not have a problem with you at this moment. I trust no one will give him a reason for that to change?" Nyx said.

"Oh no," John said.

"Then your bullying days are done?" Nyx said.

Three of them nodded rapidly.

"Most definitely."

Nyx turned to Irving and nodded at him with a smile. He still looked confused but smiled back. The bullies turned to leave.

"Wait a second. Weren't the three of you supposed to give him a gift to make up for what you've done to him?" Nyx said.

"Besides the cakes?" Irving said.

Nyx nodded. "Besides the cakes. Dessert is nice but cash

is king."

"Oh right," Steve said. He put five twenty-dollar bills on the table in front of Irving. John did the same. Steve laid a crisp hundred-dollar bill on the top.

Three bullies stood there awkwardly.

"Irving, can we go now?" Steve said.

Irving was still staring at the money. "What? Yeah, sure you can go. Is this cake stuff going to be a daily thing?"

"Do you want it to be?" Steve asked, his hands shaking.

"I don't need a cake every day. One on my birthday would be nice." Irving looked over at the girl in black. "One on Nyx's birthday too." I waved a tentacle. "Shivers, do you like chocolate cake?

I wasn't sure, so I stuck a tentacle into the nearest of the three cakes and it came out with some icing and cake which I put in my mouth. Delicious.

I nodded.

"And one on Shiver's birthday."

Irving gave them his birthday, Nyx's, then turned to me. I looked at Nyx and shrugged my tentacles. I had no idea when my birthday was. Calendars meant nothing in the Dreaming.

"Shiver's birthday is on Halloween." Nyx made up the date but it was an excellent choice.

"You shall have those cakes," Steve promised.

"And you will all sing happy birthday to Irving of course," Nyx said.

"Of course," Chuck said and the three hopefully former bullies scurried off.

"Nyx, what just happened here?"

The girl in black raised her dark eyebrows attempting to appear innocent. She couldn't pull the look off.

"First, you tell me those three won't bother me anymore. Then they show up and give me cakes and-" Irving picked up the money and counted it. "-three hundred bucks. Are you going to tell me you didn't have anything to do with this?"

"I'm going to plead the fifth on that. I could sit here and try to explain or maybe even make something up. Or…" Nyx had loaded up on eating utensils when we went through the cafeteria line. She handed a plastic fork to Irving, nine of them to me, and kept one for herself. "… we could eat cake."

Irving made the sensible choice.

We ate cake.

Patrick T. Fibbs is the pen name of author Patrick Thomas who has written over 60 books and 150 short stories. He co-created and wrote the first two books in the YA series *The Wildsidhe Chronicles.*

As Patrick T. Fibbs, he writes the *Undead Kid Dairies,* the *Babe B. Bear Mysteries, the Joy Reaper* series, and the *Ughabooz* picture books.

Patrick works as a Physical Therapist with kids in schools. He lives with his wife, 2 kids, a cat, a dog, and several imaginary friends. Patrick has also worked as a paperboy, library page, a tutor, running games in an amusement park, as a movie usher, a teacher's aide, a salesman, done phone sales and surveys as well as stocking shelves in a supermarket. He has been a DJ on the radio, an altar boy, an editor, an artist, flown an open cockpit plane, sold the shirt off of someone's back, and has been known to howl at the moon.

Please visit his website at www.PatrickTFibbs.com.

Features all

6 books in the

series in

one deluxe

volume!

NO TEACHERS. NO PARENTS.
SCHOOL IS OUT.....
OF THIS WORLD

www.talehaven.com

www.ingramcontent.com/pod-product-compliance
Lightning Source LLC
Chambersburg PA
CBHW030828200726
48285CB00007B/2393